PRAISE FOR HEATHER BLANTON

"Heather Blanton infuses her stories with immense grace and dignity."

— —LINDA BRODAY, *NEW YORK TIMES* BESTSELLING AUTHOR

"Heather Blanton is blessed with a natural story-telling ability, an 'old soul' wisdom, and wide expansive heart."

— —MARK RICHARD, EXECUTIVE PRODUCER OF AMC'S *HELL ON WHEELS*

"Fans of Louis L'Amour and Francine Rivers will find Blanton's stories even more enthralling. With wit, a clear author's voice, and storytelling chops that rival the best—you'll have found your new favorite storyteller!"

— —CARRIE FANCETT PAGELS, AWARD-WINNING AUTHOR

"Masterful at gritty fiction that points to the ultimate Creator, Heather will become one of your favorite Christian fiction authors."

— —KARI TRUMBO, *USA TODAY* BESTSELLING AUTHOR

A SCOUT FOR SKYLER

ALSO BY HEATHER BLANTON

Grace Be a Lady

ROMANCE IN THE ROCKIES SERIES

A SCOUT FOR SKYLER

HEATHER BLANTON

CKN Christian Publishing
An Imprint of Wolfpack Publishing
1707 E. Diana Street
Tampa, FL 33610

www.cknchristianpublishing.com

Paperback ISBN 979-8-89567-852-7
Ebook ISBN 979-8-89567-851-0

And Isaiah said, This sign shalt thou have of the LORD, that the LORD will do the thing that he hath spoken: shall the shadow go forward ten degrees, or go back ten degrees?

And Hezekiah answered, It is a light thing for the shadow to go down ten degrees: nay, but let the shadow return backward ten degrees.

— **2 KINGS, CHAPTER 20**

A SCOUT FOR SKYLER

PROLOGUE

Doc Owens gazed out Tobias's window at the hazy Blue Ridge Mountains and shook his head. "She won't agree, Tobias. You know how stubborn and strong-willed she is." He turned back to his patient in the bed, an older gentleman in the last stages of emphysema. "Not that I don't think it's a good idea, but she'll never agree."

The man started to speak but was cut off by a fit of coughing. Owens poured him a shot of laudanum. "Here, this will help."

Tobias took it eagerly, tossed it back, and waited a moment for the spasms to pass. "I won't be here come July. I need her squared away. She'll do anything I ask her to. Especially if it's my dyin' wish."

"But she's so...coarse. No reflection on her, she has a heart of gold, but—"

"I know I've done wrong keepin' her with me, treating her too much like a son, but she was always such a joy to be around."

"For you, maybe. I've patched up a couple of the boys in the county she's beat the hound out of. You've raised a wild

1

cat, Tobias. It's gonna take a special man to convince her to act like a female."

"I got somebody in mind."

Owens's eyes bulged. "You do? You've been giving this some thought."

"It's all I've been doing since you gave me the long face."

"Anyone I know?"

"The captain at Nate's fort."

"Oh, good Lord, not a military man. You can't expect Priscilla to go from being free as a bird and mean as a bobcat to the confined and regimented life of an army fort."

"I think she'll need a man with a strong hand, and Nate's captain, this Scotsman, has the reputation of being firm but fair."

"I hope he has also sworn off violence, because Priscilla could well drive him to it."

"Do you think I'd consider any man who wouldn't be good for my girl? I trust Nate's opinion."

"As do I, but..." Owens shoved his hands into his pockets and rocked on his heels. "Nate has never had a bad word for Corbett. And I know, for you, the sun rises and sets on Priscilla. It may not be a terrible idea. Let me write a letter to someone."

"All right, and then, if you're agreeable, I'd like you to arrange the dowry."

Doc patted his friend on the shoulder. "I'll see to it."

CHAPTER 1

PRISCILLA ROLLED UP HER BRITCHES AND DANGLED HER BARE feet off the bank into the cold creek, smiling at the pure pleasure of it. Fishing under a mid-June sun had been a chore. She wiped sweat off her forehead and grinned at the collection of trout in her basket. They were always good eating. And Pa had promised collard greens and turnips to go with them. Her stomach grumbled at the menu.

She'd seen sign of some Cherokee around, but they looked to be passing through. She'd not heard of any trouble, so she would not dwell on possibly fighting Indians today. Dinner was a nicer thought. To make sure, she scanned the sandy shore a few feet down. A wild turkey had left tracks behind, but other than that, no sign of moccasins.

"Well, how's it going, Priscilla Jones?"

She flinched at the sound of the devil's voice. Tock Howard grated on her nerves like a rooster crowing at midnight. Not only was he fat, slovenly, and foul-mouthed, he lived to pick fights with her. Pa said it was because Tock fancied her and she should give him a chance. Stop snarling at him. Maybe he would clean up and bring her flowers.

The thought sent her stomach rolling, whether Pa was joking or not.

Slowly, she climbed back up on the grass and turned expectantly.

A big man, wide, barrel-chested, wearing ratty overalls, Tock emerged from the laurel behind her and peered nosily into the basket. "Not bad. Kinda small."

She smelled the liquor on his breath. "Bigger than anything you ever catch," she shot back.

"You know that's a lie. I caught a good sixteen-inch trout last week."

"I heard about it. So has everybody in the county." She reached down and grabbed the basket of fish. "I gotta be going."

Tock laid a hand on her shoulder, holding her in place. Priscilla's mouth darn near fell open at the man's brazenness. She looked at his hand, then glared up at him.

"Listen, don't run off. I got something I want to say." Then he seemed to catch the warning in her eyes. Swallowing, he removed his hand.

"I'm in a hurry." She walked away, several feet over, to grab her cane pole leaning on a tree, but changed her mind at the last second, preferring to keep one hand free.

"Dang it, woman, I mean to say my piece."

Priscilla was already riled by Tock's hands on her. Now he was raising his voice. Slowly, she rounded on him, eyes narrowed, muscles tense. "You better have something real important on your mind, Tock, 'cause I'm fixing to teach you some manners."

He huffed and straightened to his full height. "You couldn't teach a 'coon to climb a tree. You're just a mouthy tomboy who likes to run around in britches and be the son your pa wants." He leaned toward her. "What you need is a man to straighten you out."

Tock was awfully full of himself today. Admittedly, she was a little curious as to just what was inspiring this load of manure. Moonshine or something else? "You ain't never talked to me like this. You're feeling pretty brave for some reason. I can promise you, it ain't a good enough reason."

"You know you're twenty-four years old?" He cocked his head at her like she was daft. Sweat rolled down his double-chin.

"'Course I know how old I am. How do you know?"

"You're an old maid, Priscilla." He grinned like a bear with a honeycomb. "Less you finally decided to marry me. I stopped by your place, chatted with your pa. He's on his last leg."

"You watch what you say about my pa." Before the words were even out of her mouth, Priscilla snatched her skinning knife free from her hip and threw it at Tock's head. The blade parted his hair and pinned his hat to the pine behind him.

The perfect throw pleased Priscilla immensely.

The color drained from Tock's face and he went white as grits. He gulped and reached up to touch his bare head. "You —you threw a knife at my skull."

"No, I threw it at your hat. I throw a knife at your head, you'll know it."

Suddenly, Tock flushed beet red, snatched his cap free from the tree, and spat in Priscilla's direction. "A curse on you, you ill-mannered badger. And a curse on the man who gets ya."

He thrashed off through the woods like a scalded bear, and Priscilla waited till his sounds died to retrieve her knife. "A curse on me," she muttered, rehoming the knife to its sheath. "And so what if I want to run around in britches. Ain't none of that lickspittle's business, anyhow."

She gathered up her fishing pole and headed home. With

the warm sun on her shoulders and the smell of honey-suckle in the air, her thoughts did drift, for a moment, to the future. Sometimes she longed for more than nights sitting by the fire with Pa. But he was getting old and he needed her. He'd taught her the best ways of the mountains, and she could sure provide for them both.

But he wouldn't live forever.

She shook off the thought and inhaled the fragrances of summer in the mountains. Life was good here and she was happy. That was all she'd think on for now.

FEAR SKITTERED up Priscilla's spine when she caught sight of the doc's buggy heading away from the cabin. One day, he was gonna tell her pa was dead.

"Please, not today, Lord." She jogged to the cabin, tossed her fish in the sink, and hammered on Pa's door. "Everything okay? I saw Doc Owens leaving."

The pause almost worried her, but then he spoke. "Come in, daughter."

Daughter? He always called her Prissy. That skitter of fear coming back, she entered, sat down on the bed beside him, and took his hand. "I got a passel of trout for supper. I'll fry it up just the way you like it. Plenty of pepper."

Pa clutched her hand and nodded. "Got somethin' I need to tell ya first, girl. You sit there and listen. Don't say a word till I'm done."

Priscilla squeezed his hand tighter, a knot of sadness trying to clog her throat. "All right."

"Prissy, I've done you wrong trying to keep ya for myself. I didn't want to be lonely, and you've been such a fine companion. You learned so quick everything I showed ya. Ain't nobody in the county a better shot or better hunter."

"And I'm good with my knife, too," she added, proud of scaring the spit out of Tock today.

"Yep, you sure are. But..." His face purpled as he fought against the cough, but it bubbled up in a crackly sound, stealing his breath for a moment. Priscilla knew there was nothing she could do but hold his hand and wait for it to pass.

Pa cleared his throat when the hacking died and wiped his mouth with the handkerchief he kept handy. The spells were taking more and more out of him every time they hit. "Prissy, I'm running out of time, so I'm just goin' to spit this out. I'm dying. And I want you taken care of. I'm sending you off to be the wife of an army captain out West. I hear he's a good—"

Priscilla leaped to her feet and stepped back so fast she nearly tripped over her own feet. "What?" Surely she'd heard wrong. She stuck her finger in her ear to loosen up any wax. "Lordy, it sure sounded like—"

"Not *like*. You heard me."

She lowered her hand slowly, as if she and this moment were made of glass, and if she moved too quickly, everything would shatter to pieces.

"Sit down."

"Pa," she pleaded.

"Sit down," he said gently but firmly.

She followed the command and tried to slow her racing heart. All of this was too much. She wanted to run outside and track a deer or hunt a 'coon. Do something she knew and loved. Feel the Blue Ridge Mountains beneath her bare feet.

And forget how lonely she was...

"Now, I started to say I hear he's a good man. Honest and fair. A mite hot-tempered—but I reckon you'll cure him of that. He's a man of discipline, though. That will be good for you. You ain't had enough. That's why you are wild as a buck. It's time to learn to be a lady." He looked down at his hands. "Past time. It'll make the change hard on ya, but you'll come to terms with it. Like every challenge you've ever met."

Priscilla couldn't stop the tears from coming to her eyes and they made her ashamed. She'd tried her whole life to be a good companion for her pa, because he missed Ma so much. Somewhere along the way, she'd quit trying to act like a girl and became the son he could pal around with and hunt and drink with. Now, here she was, crying like a baby. "I'm sorry, Pa. I'm sorry."

"What in the world are you sorry for?"

She sniffed and wiped her nose with the back of her leather sleeve. "I'm crying like some softheaded, addle-brained female."

Her pa sighed so heavily he sounded the most heartsick she'd ever heard.

"Lord, forgive me for my selfishness." He picked up Priscilla's hand and squeezed it between both of his. "Priscilla Jones, you are a female. And it's time to act like one. You marry this captain. You make him a good wife. And you have a passel of fine, healthy children. I'm sorry I won't be there to see them, but you'll tell them about me, won't you?"

"Oh, Pa..." Priscilla couldn't stand this pain. Fear and loss twisted her heart. Her father saying goodbye. Her future changing direction like a rabbit trail. She collapsed on his chest and he wrapped her in a warm hug.

"There, there. It will be all right. Ain't no situation yet that whooped a Jones. You promise me you'll carry through on this. It's what I'm asking from my deathbed."

Misery climbed around Priscilla's soul like a vine of poison ivy. She couldn't speak. Couldn't think. She just wanted everything to go back like it was. Even the mysterious longing in her heart was more bearable than saying goodbye to her pa.

"Promise me," he coaxed.

But there was no turning back. She nodded because she couldn't speak. At least she had time before this change happened. Didn't she? "When, Pa?" She sat up and sniffled. "When do I have to go?" Surely not before he passed on... and that might be a long time yet. Suddenly her spirits buoyed. Between now and then, maybe Pa would change his mind. She would pray he did. She would pray hard.

"I think it will be soon, darlin' girl. Soon, but I'm ready to see Jesus."

The words were like a knife in her heart. Terrified of losing him, she fell back on him and hugged him tight.

Pa patted her back. "One more thing. Wear a dress once in a while. Men like that."

THE DISPATCHES from Fort White portended a clash. Coming soon. Skyler tucked the information away in a folder and reached for a sheet of paper from his desk drawer to make his reply. He would increase the patrol size and expand the area by another ten miles. They couldn't afford to be caught by surprise by One-Who-Cries. The renegade was a menace.

He began to write but paused at the knock on his door. "Come."

Nate entered, pulling off his hat. Skyler saw right away something was wrong. The man was moving as if he had ants crawling on him. He saluted with a shaky hand. "Sir."

His voice had actually jiggled with what sounded like fear. Concerned, Skyler set down his pen. "At ease, mon. What is it?" Why was Nate being so formal? After all these years, they'd managed an informal way of working together that still retained the necessary gears of army life. Other things, such as saluting when no one was around, was something Skyler had allowed to pass.

Now he spotted sweat beading on Nate's lip. The man, impossibly pale, took a deep breath and let it out slowly. "Sir —Skyler...a woman has arrived." He paused, as if doubting it. "Yes. A woman. Um, and, well..."

Guessing now there was no real reason for concern, Skyler stood. "Spit it out. What is it?"

"She's your bride."

The words hung in the air without reply because Skyler was quite sure he'd misunderstood. After a moment of passing shock, he chuckled. "My age is catching up with me. Thirty must be when the ears go. I thought ye said bride. My bride."

"I did. That's exactly what I said."

Skyler had always prided himself on being a quick thinker, a man of action, not reaction, but he was truly at a loss. He did not comprehend Nate's words. Perhaps this was a joke? "Are ye toying with me, lad?" His voice dropped to a somber, warning level. "Pray to God ye're toying with me." If this was no joke, someone was going to die.

"The...lady has letters. From her father...and yours."

Suddenly, Skyler felt as if his legs had hollowed out and they were about to snap under his weight. A bride? This was absurd. But his father...his meddlesome, manipulative, mischievous father, was not past this sort of thing. He'd been after Skyler almost from the moment of Louisa's death to think of Bea and remarry.

Skyler half-sat, half-fell into his chair. "A bride. My bride."

"Yes, sir, that's what she said."

Skyler was thunderstruck. Nate seemed to recover his wits and strode over to the small bar in the corner. "Here, this will have to help." He poured a snort of whiskey and handed it to Skyler.

Skyler drank it without thinking and the liquor did burn off a little of the shock. He rose and studied his friend, who appeared to have regained some of his normal composure. His fidgeting had stopped and his color had returned.

"Might I suggest you meet the...lady?" Nate said.

"Why do ye keep pausing like that? Is there something amiss with the lass?" All kinds of horrible possibilities flooded Skyler's mind. The girl was hugely obese. Toothless. God forbid, English? Now anger rose up in him. It would be like his father to make a huge joke out of something as serious as bringing a woman to the fort. "She's horrible on the eyes, is she?"

Nate stepped back from the desk and scratched his forehead. "Maybe not, cleaned up a little, but..."

"I'm growing ill with ye, Nate. What is it?"

"She's in buckskins."

"Ye mean, like a squaw?" He'd kill his father for thinking this was fun—

"No, I mean like a warrior. Knife. Moccasins...britches."

"Britches." Skyler sat down again. Hard. "Britches." He contemplated the situation and the choice words he would be telegraphing Lord Corbett. A telegraph followed by a lass in moccasins, sent right back from whence she came. Yes, that was it. He'd simply send her back and move on with his business.

A plan devised, Skyler stood again. "I'll make this quick."

"She gave me these." Nate pulled two sealed envelopes

from his jacket and handed them to Skyler. "Would you prefer to read them first?"

Skyler knew the handwriting on the first one immediately. Large, bold, perfect. His father's handwriting. The other, shaky, some of the letters were formed incorrectly, was not familiar. Both envelopes were addressed to Captain Corbett.

Skyler tapped them on his desk and sighed. "So, where did ye say she is?"

"In your parlor. I thought that was...more discreet. I instructed her to wait."

He started opening the envelope from his father. "Give me a moment, then."

CHAPTER 2

Dear son,
I've arranged for a very special gift. A bit rough around the edges it is, but I've no doubt your military background and leadership skills will enable you to manage it.
Love,
Da

Skyler nearly crumpled the letter. It dripped with irony and mirth. So typical of his father. He opened the next envelope and grimaced at the shaky handwriting, as if the one-page letter had been written by a very elderly gentleman.

Dear Captain Corbett,
On the good word of my neighbor, Jed Owens, and his son, Nathaniel, I understand you are in need of a wife. The Owens men tell me you are fair,

honorable, and decent. I hereby send my daughter Priscilla to you. She is skilled with a gun and a knife. She tracks both man and animal better than any person here in Ocoee County. She is strong and hard-working. I admit to an absence of book learning for her, but she can read some and is very teachable. She has a quick wit and a quick mind.

She is the most valuable thing in the world to me, but if you are reading this, then I have passed out of it. I leave Priscilla in your care. I pray you will be kind and patient with her. I reckon I know she is a little rough around the edges, but your father says you make men out of boys. Making a wife out of Priscilla should be easy for you, then.

God bless you.

Tobias Jones

"Good Lord," Skyler whispered, stunned at this turn of events. The clock on the wall ticked off the seconds, mocking him. He had to face— "Wait..." he scanned the letter again. "Nathaniel Owens?" Skyler surged to his feet and bellowed, "Lieutenant!"

Nate scrambled inside and stopped in front of Skyler's desk, ramrod straight. "Yes, sir?"

"Ye knew?" He waved the letter. "Ye knew?"

"I—I knew? Knew what?"

Skyler read aloud, "On the good word of my neighbor, Jed Owens, and his son, Nathaniel...I understand ye are in need of a wife. The Owens men tell me you are fair, honorable, and decent." He tossed the letter to his desk. "Explain."

Nate closed his eyes as if recalling a horrible experience. "Skyler, I'm sorry. When I was home last, of course my father asked after you. I told him I thought you were coming along well since Louisa's death. A neighbor was there for some of the conversation. I—I certainly didn't imply—"

"My father. How did my father get involved in this?"

Nate licked his lips. "I can only assume my father wrote to him."

Fury coursed through Skyler like boiling water. How dare any of these men presume to choose a wife for him. He slammed his fist into his desk. "This will not stand."

CRACKING THE KITCHEN DOOR A HAIR, Bea Corbett watched the strange visitor in the parlor. It took her a moment to realize the person in the buckskin shirt and leather britches was female. How astonishing.

Surely she's a scout. Oh, I wonder if that is Calamity Jane. Wouldn't that be exciting?

Bea pondered the idea a moment and decided firmly that this odd person now wiggling her *bare* toes in the Persian rug was most assuredly the famous Calamity Jane. Probably here to give Da a report on the Indians.

If only she were here to stay a bit and distract Da, Bea lamented. She was tired of him watching her every move. What was wrong with five minutes in the barn with Henry Willoughby? He was so handsome and sweet...

Bea daydreamed about kissing him, letting him hold her hand. Her da would kill them both, of course, but just being near Henry made Bea's heart sing. And she wanted every opportunity to be near him.

She peered a little closer at the woman drifting over to the piano. She had a pretty face. Her hair was an attractive shade of gold. And she was slender but curvy. Buckskins didn't hide the fact she was female, just roughed it up a little.

Could she distract Da? If she was staying around for a little while? Only one way to find out...

PRISCILLA COULDN'T HELP HERSELF. In spite of the jitters about what was to come, she kicked off her moccasins and let her feet sink into the colorful rug. *It's so soft.* She wiggled her toes. *Mighty nice on a cold day, I bet.*

She hugged her satchel against her chest and surveyed the pretty little parlor. Nicer and bigger than Pastor Holbrook's back in Ocoee. Delicate furniture was sprinkled around the sunny room. Sure was different from the preacher's dark, rugged cabin. This room was light and airy. Polished wood glistened in the sun. She spied the piano over in the corner and nearly gasped.

In awe of it, she wandered up slowly and clucked her tongue. "Sure is a big one," she whispered.

"May I help you?"

Priscilla whirled toward the voice. A young girl with flowing, curly red hair blinked at her with wide, blue eyes. "Lord have mercy," Priscilla yelped. "You snuck up on me quieter than a Cherokee."

"You did look rather absorbed." She flicked a glance at Priscilla's bare feet.

"I ain't never seen such a nice room." She side-stepped back over to her shoes and slipped into them, embarrassed she'd been surprised and caught barefoot. "Never seen a rug like this before, either."

"It's a Persian carpet." The girl surveyed Priscilla head-to-toe and back again. Suddenly, the buckskins felt too warm and uncomfortable. "Are you Calamity Jane?" she asked, sounding as if she hoped Priscilla might say yes.

"No."

"Are you one of our scouts, maybe? I didn't know they let women do that."

"I scouted pretty regular for the Ocoee County militia. But that ain't why I'm here now."

The girl frowned, as if Priscilla vexed her. "Ain't isn't a word."

"If that's so, how come I can say it?"

The frown melted into a half-smile. "I meant to say it isn't proper English. Why are you here?"

"You Captain Corbett's daughter, by chance?"

"I am."

Priscilla exhaled heavily, puttering her lips. "Reckon I'm to be your new ma. You talk funny."

The girl shook her head as if she didn't catch it all. "What in the world do you mean *my new ma?*" She said the last trying to copy the way Priscilla talked, but with her strange accent, it almost hurt Priscilla's ears.

"My pa, your grandpa, and I guess your pappy got together and decided I should marry him. Apparently he's in need of a wife."

The girl took a step back and her mouth fell open. Priscilla could see the wheels turning in her head and waited for things to settle one way or the other before she said anything else. Suddenly, the girl busted out laughing and extended her hand to Priscilla. "Oh, forgive me. I am Bea Corbett." The two women shook hands. "And if you think I talk funny, wait till you hear Da—ooow."

"Sorry." Priscilla had given Bea a good, hearty handshake but it was too much for the delicate thing, and she pulled her hand back a little embarrassed.

Bea wiggled her fingers, as if making sure they weren't all broken. "Quite the grip you've got."

A little self-conscious, Priscilla let her satchel slip to the ground and she brushed the front of her buckskin shirt. "Chop a lot of wood, that happens."

"Yes...um, well, you need to meet Da."

A sly little smile played on the girl's lips and Priscilla, not being blind, chose to call her on it. "Somethin' funny?"

"Da didn't know you were coming, did he?"

"I don't know. I kinda think now maybe not. That fella, Lieutenant Owens, seemed awfully surprised at my arrival."

And this gave Priscilla even more cause for concern. She'd thought Pa, Doc Owens, and Lord Corbett had squared things with the captain. The meeting was already going to be awkward enough, but if the man had no idea to expect her...she looked down at her britches, then at the pretty, lacy dress the girl was wearing. Priscilla didn't have anything as fine as that. Just two simple dresses, one muslin, one cotton. "You reckon I should change into a dress?"

"No," Bea said quickly. "I think you should meet my father exactly the way you are. After all, Shakespeare said, 'to thine own self be true.'"

"Shakespeare. He a friend of yours?"

"Shakespeare was—"

Rapid thumping on the front porch stopped the girl in mid-sentence and alerted Priscilla that she was about to meet her groom. A jumble of butterflies took flight in her stomach.

"Oh, there's Da now."

The front door swung in with frightening force and a handsome man in a blue uniform burst into the house like a summer storm. Priscilla noted his thick, silky hair, the color of honey in the sun, and blazing eyes. Blue as an October sky, they were. Pretty, but full of fire, and they froze her in place.

Then she realized that fire was aimed at her.

He stormed toward her, and for the first time in her life, Priscilla almost backed up from a fight. Almost. He charged up within a few feet, then stopped abruptly and took in her appearance. "Dear God. My father has sent me a savage."

The barb cut Priscilla, much to her surprise. Her pride bleeding, she sneered at the captain. "Better a savage than a dandy."

His brow shot up. "Worse. A savage with no respect."

"Ain't seen nothing to respect...yet."

The two of them glared at each other. Behind the captain, the lieutenant softly shut the door and approached the spitting, hissing pair. "Um, Captain Corbett, may I present Miss Priscilla Jones."

"Your wife, Da," Bea sang, grinning wide and sly, like a fox with a chick in its mouth. Priscilla understood she had no friends in this room.

Well, she knew fighting better than peacemaking. She raised her chin but couldn't think of anything to say.

Captain Corbett ran a hand over his mouth, then proceeded to walk a circle around Priscilla. "This must be the most extraordinary joke my da has ever played on me." Suddenly, the man threw back his head and laughed, a rich, hearty sound that almost made Priscilla laugh. Confused glances bounced around from the Lieutenant to Priscilla to Bea and back.

Captain Corbett slapped the lieutenant in the ribs, still laughing. "Now, I see. My father has too much time and money on his hands. I'll admit, it's a grand joke."

The tense expressions on Lieutenant Owens and Bea's faces reflected Priscilla's feelings. This was no joke. She did not take to being examined like livestock and then laughed at, to boot. "I ain't funnin' you, Captain. And I reckon you'd best stop laughing 'fore I box your ears."

The captain laughed harder for another few seconds, until he apparently sensed the actual seriousness of the situation. Then all his good humor evaporated like smoke. "You dress and talk like—like that"—he waved his hand over her —"on purpose?"

"*You* talk like that on purpose, you pompous—?" Priscilla bit her tongue. Literally. This man hurt her feelings and infuriated her all in the same instant. "My pa's dying wish was for me to come here and be a good wife to you." Emotion tightened her throat and she fought it back. "I'll do my best." She glanced again at Bea and her petite mannerisms wrapped up in the pretty, feminine dress. "Sorry if I ain't what you'd pick for yourself. I reckon they could have told you a little bit more about me."

"This is no prank?" Captain Corbett looked at the lieutenant. "This is no joke? The letters. They're real?"

"Yes, sir, I believe so."

Captain Corbett stepped back a few feet as if the movement would help him see Priscilla better. "Forgive me, Miss Jones, I dinnae mean to be rude. However, ye are right. They certainly could have given me more information. Starting with the fact that ye were on yer way here. Now, I am not looking for a wife, and if I were, a backwoods waif in men's britches…" His gaze switched to Bea, and he trailed off. She looked appalled at his words. Tugging on his collar, the captain cleared his throat. "Well, what I mean to say is, ye're welcome to get back on the stage."

"Ya mean you don't want me?" For some unfathomable reason, this possibility had not entered Priscilla's brain. Oh, she'd accepted the husband might not like her, much less love her, but she'd thought any man would want a woman to cook and clean for him. In her case, even hunt and fight for him.

"I have rampaging renegades moving into our patrol area. I dinnae have time for a wife. Please be on your way." He turned to go.

Priscilla...was at a loss. What was she supposed to do now? She'd given Pa her word, but the man didn't want her. Didn't that release her from her promise? But what the heck was she gonna do if she didn't stay?

"Uh, Captain Corbett," Lieutenant Owens began, intercepting him at the door. "There is one problem."

"Only one?" the captain snipped.

"The stage line is closed. At least for a few days. An attack on the way station at Crazy Woman Creek. The scout just made it in."

Captain Corbett ran his hand through his hair. "Report."

"Two casualties. All the horses were stolen. Our patrol is already after them."

Captain Corbett spun back around to Priscilla. He opened his mouth to speak, waved his hand in a sign of surrender, and glared at his daughter. "Put her in the guest room, Bea." Over his shoulder, he yelled, "And see that she gets a bath."

CHAPTER 3

WHEN THE CAPTAIN STORMED FROM HIS HOUSE, A SILENCE fell that reminded Priscilla of the stillness after a loud and violent thunderstorm. It always took nature a few minutes to recover. She felt just like that now. She sure hadn't come West to be treated like a farmhand—no, a farm *animal*.

"Your pa ain't got no manners," she said flatly.

Bea bit her bottom lip and nodded. "He can be very abrupt. He doesn't realize how he hurts people's feelings."

Priscilla raised her chin defiantly. "He didn't hurt my feelings. I was just expecting a warmer welcome, was all."

"Well, you are a bit of a shock. No one knew you were coming. Other than Grand Da, apparently."

"Yeah, that seemed to set your pa off, too."

"My grandfather is mischievous. He's always playing odd jokes on my father. Last month, he sent him a stuffed rabbit with antlers. Said it was jackalope."

"A rabbit with antlers? Ain't no such thing."

"Yes, I suppose that was the point. Well, let's get you settled and then we'll work on the bath."

Priscilla shook her head and nibbled on her bottom lip. "I don't know. I ain't so sure I'm staying."

"I thought you said it was your father's dying wish for you to be here."

"Yeah, but if your pa don't want me, don't that kind of release me from my promise?"

"Perhaps. Do you think you should give up so easily, though?"

Priscilla narrowed her eyes on the little gal. Something wasn't right here. "Why do you care so much if I stay or go?"

Bea clasped her fingers behind her back and shrugged. "Da is lonely. My mother has been gone over a year now. She was sick a year before that, and...well, I think we should move on. She wanted us to. She said so."

"Hmm. Sorry about your ma. I lost mine when I was eight."

"I was glad when she passed. I know that sounds awful, but she was in so much pain, and she was so weak."

"No, that don't sound bad. You wanted her at peace. Was your ma a Believer?"

"A Believer? Do you mean a Christian?"

"Uh-huh."

"Yes, she was. Very much so."

"Are you?"

"Yes."

"Then you'll see her again."

"I believe that. My father—well, he's still angry with God. *Very* angry, so don't bring up religion to him."

A nudge in Priscilla's spirit pushed her toward something. But she needed to be sure. "Soon as I set my bag in the room, I'd like to take a walk. Then the bath, if that's all right with you."

"Of course. Right this way."

Priscilla watched the way the girl picked up her skirt and

sashayed toward the steps like a princess. Priscilla was pretty sure she herself did not walk that way. She'd learned to take big, bold strides to keep up with Pa. And then with all the men in the county.

"Coming?" Bea asked from the bottom step.

"Yes, ma'am." Priscilla picked up her satchel and tried slower, smaller steps.

"YE SWEAR ye knew nothing about this?" Skyler asked as he and Nate charged across the parade ground back to his office.

"This?"

"A bride coming today."

"I swear today is a surprise."

Skyler was actually relieved at the scout's report of trouble, though he lamented the loss of life at Crazy Woman Creek. Somewhere beneath the mask of Priscilla Jones's buckskin britches and saucy tongue, he'd seen the hint of a pretty young woman. It disturbed him greatly that he'd noticed.

A man would have to be blind not to appreciate her shimmering blonde hair hanging in a long braid, the gentle curve of her hip where her knife perched, and green eyes flashing with temper. She was a picture.

She was also a hellion. An ill-tempered, poorly educated, sassy wench. What could his father have been thinking? A woman like that was more dangerous to a man than a horde of screaming Indians.

He thundered up the steps, fleetingly saluted his sentry, and burst in on the scout. So covered in dust he was barely recognizable, he stood and saluted. A short, stout member of the Ute tribe, he'd proven a reliable scout. Skyler returned the salute and surveyed the man. Blood smeared his left sleeve.

"Broken Kettle, you ran into some trouble?"

"A Cheyenne named Black Elk and two of his warriors attacked us near the stage stop at Crazy Woman. He let me live to bring you a message."

"Oh?" The arrogance of these renegades. "What is it?"

"Send no more scouts after One-Who-Cries. If you do, they will not return."

"Understood. Thank ye for the report."

Broken Kettle rose, offered a weary salute, and shuffled out the door. Skyler suspected he would not see the Ute again.

CHAPTER 4

Priscilla and Bea strolled down the boardwalk of Rose Creek, the town that had sprung up around Fort Logan. The place was busy. Wagon after wagon rumbled along the street, loaded with dry goods and settlers headed west. Miners led mules along, their packs loaded with clanking, banging tools and tin pans that filled the summer air with a kind of music. The boardwalk flowed with a steady stream of cowboys, soldiers, and a few women.

All of them glanced pointedly at Priscilla or outright stared for a second. "Why do folks keep looking at me like I got two heads?" She'd noticed this behavior in Dodge City, as well, when the stage had stopped overnight. The men whose stares lingered the longest made her the most uncomfortable. Made her feel like she'd left open the back door on her long johns.

"I believe it's your clothing. Here...well, a woman in buckskins, much less britches, is probably something they've never seen before."

Priscilla drifted her fingers over the beading on her shirt. "A simple, thin dress like you got on just doesn't hold up to real chores." She used to wear a dress to church, but then she got out of even that habit.

"Do you have any dresses with you?"

"Two."

"Oh, if you stay, we'll have to go shopping for more." The girl slid a sneaky gaze over at Priscilla. "You know, you're very pretty. And shapely. I'm sure that's also a reason some men are staring."

As if to prove her point, two cowboys walked past them, tipping their hats. Priscilla saw the polite appreciation in their eyes for Bea, then shock at Priscilla. But as they walked on, she could feel their gazes linger on her backside. "Hmm," she grunted.

"Was there anything in particular you wanted to see in Rose Creek?"

Priscilla looked around at the busy town. She'd hoped for a private, quiet spot by a river, but one didn't seem handy. "I'd like a few minutes in a church. Got a decision to make. Need to talk to the Lord about it."

"Oh, that's fine. We have two. A Baptist church and a Catholic mission."

"Reckon the Baptist will do."

PRISCILLA SAT on the front pew in the empty church and gazed up at the old wooden cross. Hanging on the back wall, sunlight poured in on it, as if spotlighting it just for her. She clucked her tongue with a sigh and looked out the window. Bea sat on a swing, fidgeting, spinning, waiting on Priscilla.

"Well, this is some mess, Lord. I don't want to be here. Captain Corbett don't want me here. I don't reckon Pa planned on that when he set this up. So, what would You have me do?"

Honor thy father and thy mother so that it will be well with you and your days will be many.

"Yes, sir, I've thought of that. It's why I'm here. Trying to honor Pa. And I ain't looking for the easy way out, but the captain ain't on board with things." Again, her gaze drifted out to Bea. "She's a Believer, but for how long, if her pa don't believe in You? Worse, he's angry at You. Probably blames You for taking his wife."

She closed her eyes and laced her fingers. "I ain't never run from a fight or a calling, Lord. When You've led me to somebody who needed to hear the gospel, I've tried to tell them. But Captain Corbett, my lands, the anger comes off him like heat from a buck stove. He almost kinda scares me." His blue eyes, full of fire, rose up in her mind.

Fear thou not, for I am with thee: be not dismayed, for I am thy God: I will strengthen thee, yea, I will help thee...

She swallowed, getting the direction she'd suspected the moment Bea had told her of her father's fight with the Lord. "All right, Lord. I'll give it my best shot."

BEA LEANED her cheek on the swing's rope and stared off at nothing. Traffic flowed at a steady pace on the distant street, but all she could see was her handsome, dreamy Henry Willoughby. She'd first noticed him chopping wood out back of her father's office. He'd been working without his shirt. Sweat gleamed on his broad shoulders. He'd smiled and said, "Hey, kiddo. Want to help me stack?"

She thought that if he'd known she was the captain's daughter, the invitation might never have happened, and she'd delayed telling him this as long as possible. In fact, she'd only admitted it the day she'd followed him into the barn. Shoveling and mucking and feeding, he'd offered no reaction other than to say he liked Captain Corbett. He struck him as very capable. And then he'd once more called her *kiddo* and asked her to hand him a curry comb.

Bea frowned. *It's almost as if he doesn't see me as a woman. Why, I'm fourteen. Maybe he is scared of Da and doesn't want to show it.*

Her rumination was interrupted by Priscilla bouncing out of the church. A strange creature, Bea thought. Dressing like a man, not only hiding her beauty, but she actually seemed unaware of how pretty she was. And so sorely lacking in education and manners.

But fearless. Bea had liked very much the way the woman had fired right back at Da about respect. He tended to roll over people who let him. If yelling didn't cow them, his rank did.

Miss Priscilla Jones, however, was not in the army, nor did she cow easily, or so it would appear. If she stayed around, things could be very interesting in their household. Only, she wasn't sure she really wanted this woman to be her stepmother.

Good Lord, look at her. Swaggering toward me in pants. Pants. And she doesn't even know who William Shakespeare is.

Bea rose from the swing, deciding that, entertaining or not, this woman was too embarrassing to be seen with. On the other hand...if she could be a problem for Da, he might forget about Bea for a bit.

"Well, I got me an answer," Priscilla said, walking up and leaning on the tree that hosted the swing.

"And?"

"If your pa will allow it, I'll stay. And I'm ready for a bath now."

"All right." Bea didn't know how she felt about this, but

hoped it would be to her advantage. "Well, let's take a shortcut home and we'll get you cleaned up."

Bea led them the back way, which cut out one whole block, but would have them traipsing behind Madam Orr's House. Which was next door to the Five Cactus Saloon. And they'd have to skirt some shanties, but it was broad daylight. Bea had never had any trouble, though she'd noticed a couple of shady characters watching her once from the back stoop of Madam Orr's. She'd vowed then she wouldn't repeat the route alone.

PLANNING to stay didn't mean Priscilla had all the answers yet. Captain Corbett might refuse and she'd have to leave. Or, what if she did stay? What exactly was she going to do?

This question brought her attention back to her surroundings. *Some things must be the same the world over,* she thought, scanning the short row of shanties on one side and the saloon and house of ill-repute on the other. The homes belonged to folks who were either lazy and had no mind for improving their lot or who had no time for God. But they had time for drinking and fornicating.

Up ahead two men emerged from one of the shanties, passing a bottle between them, and they paused when they spotted the girls. The hair rose up on the back of Priscilla's neck. "I don't think much of your shortcut." There was no choice but to proceed past the pair or turn around. Priscilla shifted places with Bea, putting herself between the girl and the men. "If I say run," she whispered out of the side of her mouth, "you skedaddle. You hear me?"

"What? I can't leave—"

"You'll run, and you'll run fast as you can."

Bea bit off whatever else she was going to say as they

came within ten or so feet of the men. Priscilla kept her gaze straight ahead and prayed the girl would, too. These kinds of men, like bears, took eye contact as a challenge.

"Howdy, la—" one of them started but paused as his gaze traveled over Priscilla. "Well, looky here, Fred. It's Calamity Jane."

Priscilla took Bea's elbow but kept their pace the same and her gaze straight ahead.

The men scowled, though, when the girls didn't acknowledge them. "We're talking to you," one of them said, gravel and anger in his voice.

"We're just passing through, gents. Don't want no trouble."

The two moved quickly to cut off Priscilla and Bea. The girl gasped and Priscilla put her arm in front of her.

"Yeah, well," one of the men said, raising the bottle of whiskey, "we want to talk to you. Have a drink with us."

"Sorry, the girl and I are in a hurry." She directed Bea to the right, attempting to go around the men. "Maybe some other time."

The men, however, blocked them once more. "Boy, howdy, I ain't never seen a female in britches." He whistled as he scanned Priscilla up one side and down the other. "They don't even dress like that in Madam Orr's."

Bea's fingers on Priscilla's squeezed desperately tight. Priscilla didn't know what made her the maddest. The manners of these two drunk goats or the fear they were inflicting on the little girl. Either way, they needed a lesson in manners.

"Bea, you remember what I said?"

"Yes, ma'am."

"Do it." To her credit, the girl bolted like a bear cub leaping after a trout. One of the men moved to stop her, but

Priscilla stepped in front of him and smiled sweetly. "Now, let the little thing go on. She's just a minnow."

The man frowned but then apparently reconsidered things. Once more, he scanned Priscilla, making it almost impossible for her to hold back a sneer. She just needed to give Bea another few seconds.

The man relaxed and nodded. "Sure." He smacked his buddy in the ribs. "I ain't no cradle-robber."

"Yeah, she needs another few years." His friend agreed, offering the bottle to Priscilla. "Got time now for a little socializing?" he asked, licking his lips and looking her over like she was a hog on a spit.

Priscilla smiled just as sweetly as she could and took the whiskey. "I'll make time."

CHAPTER 5

BEA RAN SO FAST THAT SHE COULDN'T FEEL THE GROUND beneath her feet. *Da. Get Da.* She was nearly blind with panic. *What are those two men going to do to Miss Jones?*

She emerged on the street, skidded to a stop, then immediately turned toward the fort. Tears blurred her vision as she scrambled toward her father's office. The sentries at the gate saw her coming and immediately rushed to meet her.

"Miss Bea, you all right?" Sergeant Bonhoeffer asked, concern etched in his scruffy, weathered face.

"I need Da. My friend's in trouble."

"I just saw him." He grabbed her hand and ran with her. "He's at the blacksmith."

For an older fellow, he was swift and nearly dragged Bea. They burst into the forge as the blacksmith was just stepping back from Da's horse. Her father was there, holding the reins, and he saw her fear instantly.

"Lass, what is it?"

She freed herself from the sergeant and ran to him. "Help Miss Jones." Bea ground her teeth to keep back a sob. "Two men. Behind Madam Orr's. She told me to run."

Her father never hesitated. He rounded on his horse, stepped into the stirrup, and was exiting the barn before his bum was in the saddle. To her amazement, Sergeant Bonhoeffer grabbed a bare horse from a nearby stall, leaped onto its back, and shot after her father, the horse a streak of black lightning lunging into the sunlight.

Bea had never seen men move so fast. And she was proud. Proud of her father for believing her and rising to the emergency. Proud of Sergeant Bonhoeffer for not even bothering with tack to follow his commanding officer.

"Cavalry," Mr. Blackwell muttered from behind her. "Showoffs."

Bea's grin widened. "Yes." But the expression turned upside down as she thought of Miss Jones, still in the alley with those two horrible, frightening men.

SKYLER HEARD the sound of hooves behind him but never slowed. He knew one of his men was riding with him. They flew through the gate, pounded down Main Street, turned abruptly at Madam Orr's, and emerged onto the back alley.

He pulled his horse to a sudden, dirt-spraying stop and simultaneously fought to keep his mouth from falling open.

One man lay on the ground, unconscious, a shattered whiskey bottle by his head. And Miss Jones sat atop another man, holding a knife to his throat. His hands were splayed out beside him in complete surrender.

Sergeant Bonhoeffer drew up beside him. "What the devil?"

Aye, Skyler thought. *The devil indeed.*

"Y'all here to take these varmints off my hands?" she asked over her shoulder.

Neither Skyler nor the sergeant moved for a moment,

then they both seemed to shake off the shock and dismounted. They drew their guns and Miss Jones slowly extricated herself from the downed man. He looked at her, eyes round with fear, then filled with relief as the two military men approached.

"Miss Jones," Skyler said evenly, his revolver pointed at the man, though he wondered if this was the correct target. "Explain."

"This fella and his buddy there approached me and your daughter." She returned her knife to its sheath as she talked. "I believe they had nefarious intentions and so I told her to run. I figured she'd fetch help quick. Though the two of 'em weren't much trouble."

"Do you mean to say," Sergeant Bonhoeffer said, disbelief evident in his voice, "you took down these two men yourself?"

"Got the jump on 'em. It wasn't too hard after that." She cut her eyes at Skyler. A glimmering green, they burned hot with her anger. "They scared your daughter. That made me kinda mad. Worthless lickspittles."

Skyler jerked his gaze to the man climbing to his feet and the other still lying unconscious. His own anger mixed with relief.

"How come you bash him in the head?" the sergeant asked.

"Yeah," the man who'd been at the wrong end of the knife said. "She's crazy. We didn't do nothing. Just invited her to have a drink with us."

"You scared the girl," Miss Jones snapped. Skyler saw her hand go to the hilt of her knife again. "And you wouldn't let me pass. You're fortunate I've a few things on my mind or I might would've whittled a hole in your head."

The man backed up a step, as if she still might. Skyler was stunned at the fear she'd thrown into him. Miss Jones truly was a hellion. The man on the ground still hadn't moved, and Skyler wondered if he was alive. "Sergeant, keep him covered." He then moved to check on the unconscious victim. When he touched him, the man groaned. Skyler breathed a sigh of relief.

He stood and holstered his weapon and glared at the other man. "Miss Jones is claiming self-defense. My daughter ran to the fort, terrified out of her mind, which, as you can imagine, dinnae please me."

"I swear, captain, we didn't touch her. We wouldn't have hurt no little girl. And we saw this one here, paradin' around in britches. We thought…well, we thought—"

"You thought what?" Miss Jones demanded, stomping up to the man.

Out of instinct, Skyler pulled her back and out of Sergeant Bonhoeffer's line of fire.

"Well…" The man motioned to her body. "You ain't dressed like a lady. And them britches don't hide nothing."

Miss Jones gasped and turned as pink as a sunset. Behind them, the man on the ground groaned and began slowly climbing to his feet. Skyler nudged Miss Jones out of the way and spoke to the first victim. "I'm wroth with any man who would accost my daughter. Since it seems ye both got your comeuppance, I'll let this drop. Mind ye"—he raised a warning finger—"if we cross paths again, it will nae be to your benefit. Ye ken my meaning?"

The man raised his hands. "There won't be any more trouble."

Skyler returned to his horse and mounted. Then he extended a hand to Miss Jones. Her eyes bugged, then she nodded and lit into the saddle with the agility of a deer.

As Sergeant Bonhoeffer backed up to his horse, still pointing his gun at Miss Jones's victim, the man motioned toward her. "That your new scout, Captain? Best keep her on a leash, or she's liable to start a war."

Miss Jones shifted as if she might leap from the saddle. "Why you—"

Skyler pressed a firm hand down on her knee. "Be quiet, woman."

He felt her body stiffen up behind him like rawhide drying in the sun. As they rode away from the alley, Skyler wondered if, indeed, he had found a housekeeper and a bodyguard for his daughter. She'd proven herself capable in the one area, and he was grateful. Then he wondered how Miss Jones had found herself in the alley behind the brothel.

"Just what were ye and Bea doing back here?"

"She said it was a shortcut. Seein' as how I don't have the lay of the land yet, I didn't question."

Dear God, what if Bea had come this way by herself? In spite of his simmering fury over this whole situation, Skyler had the presence of mind to thank her. "What ye did for Bea. Telling her to run. That was very foolish but brave of ye. Thank ye."

He felt her shrug. "T'wern't nothin. They was drunk, and I don't think they meant any real harm."

Skyler glanced over at the sergeant, riding the black horse without any tack, and nodded his approval. He had some fine soldiers under his command. They made him proud.

If only Miss Jones were a man, he thought, *if only.*

To Priscilla's great shock, Bea threw herself into her arms and wailed like a banshee. "Oh, Miss Jones, I thought they'd killed you...or-or worse."

Bewildered by the reaction, Priscilla patted the girl on

the back. "Now, no need for all this cryin'. You fetched your pa and he saved me."

She met Captain Corbett's eyes over the top of the girl's head. He cleared his throat and looked away. "Yes, well…" He drifted around to the other side of the desk and sat down. "Everything is fine, Bea. Do ye think ye could manage to go home and start dinner? Miss Jones will be along."

Bea peeked at him through her mussed-up tangle of red curls and Priscilla's disheveled braid. "She will?" She sniffled and straightened up. "Will she be staying?"

"Aye. She has to for a few days. There is no stage until we clear the area of renegades."

This seemed to dampen Bea's mood a little, but she hugged Priscilla again and stepped back. "I'll go draw you a bath. How does that sound?"

Priscilla understood the peace offering and nodded. "That sounds fine."

As Bea was leaving, Lieutenant Owens met her in the door and clutched her chin in a brotherly way. "Are you all right, Bea? I heard there was some trouble."

"I'm fine. Thank you." And she dashed on her way.

The lieutenant looked dissatisfied with the answer, as evidenced by a furrowed brow, but shut the door behind him. When he turned, he surveyed Priscilla and Captain Corbett with a raised eyebrow. "Sergeant Bonhoeffer is telling quite a story, sir."

Captain Corbett cursed under his breath. "What exactly is the mon saying?"

"For one thing, that Miss Jones here put down two ruffians in town." He looked at Priscilla, studied her, but not in the way the men in the alley had. Something in his expression almost said he believed that part of the story. "And that she's our new scout."

40

"Blast," the captain muttered. "Rumors. Rumors in a fort are like a prairie fire. Make sure everyone knows she is not our new scout."

"Yes, sir."

Then the captain turned those breath-stealing blue eyes on Priscilla. They rattled her so, she'd nearly dropped her knife in the alley earlier. His jaw moved back and forth for several seconds, as if he had a ton of words but couldn't get any of them out. Finally, he shook his head. "Woman, I'll expect two things by this evening."

Priscilla didn't like the way he called her *woman*. Like he was saying *slave* or *dog*. "I expect something right here and right now."

The man's eyebrows rose clear to his honey-brown hairline. "Oh, by all means, please share."

Priscilla felt her face flush as her jaw tightened. Captain Corbett could make a preacher cuss. *Oh, Lord, this is a tall order, but I can't let him run over me...* "I expect you to talk to me with respect. I ain't no dog."

Out of the corner of her eye, she could see Lieutenant Owens fighting a smile. He crossed his arms and pressed a hand to his mouth.

Captain Corbett slapped his hand on his desk and leaped to his feet. "Well, when ye don't smell like one—"

"Captain Corbett," Lieutenant Owens butted in. "Your two conditions, sir."

The captain's glare would have melted weaker men, but Priscilla got the impression the tall, easy-going lieutenant was used to his captain's ornery ways.

"You have business to attend," Lieutenant Owens said more softly. "I'm sure you don't want to spend all day..." He trailed off and nodded in her direction.

Fussing at Priscilla?

Captain Corbett huffed mightily and moved his glare

from his officer to Priscilla. After a moment, he smiled, but it was cold and forced. "After yer *bath*"—he emphasized the word—"if ye would help Bea with dinner, that would be appreciated. Your Highness."

Priscilla imagined tossing her knife. An easy throw right down the middle of those pretty waves of honey-colored hair, sticking the blade in the map behind his head. Instead, she merely nodded and returned the cold, hard smile. "It would be my pleasure, Captain."

PRISCILLA WAS a little suspicious of the fast way Lieutenant Owens volunteered to escort her to the captain's home. As they strode off the porch and across the parade ground, though, her attention drifted to the men watching her. Too many of them reminded her of the men in the alley. Suddenly, she felt like she had no britches on at all and tried to hurry the lieutenant along by picking up her speed.

"How long you known the captain, Lieutenant?" she asked conversationally.

"Oh, let's see, about fifteen years."

"Your pa said you spoke highly of him. That's one reason I'm here."

"About that. Just what did my father tell you about me... uh, and I mean, Captain Corbett?"

"Not enough. Not near enough."

The lieutenant bit down a smile. Or at least tried. "He's a bit gruff."

"Surly like a grizzly bear with a sore paw."

Lieutenant Owens seemed to think about that for a minute, then he nodded. "I think that's about right. Only, the sore paw is his heart. He's not allowed himself to recover from losing Louisa."

"Bea mentioned it. Said her pa is some angry with God over the loss."

"Captain Corbett takes issue with anything—man or beast—that he can't control."

"Sorry way to live. Leads to a lot of disappointment, I reckon."

"I reckon, too." They walked a few feet in silence before Lieutenant Owens started talking again. "He's my dear friend. I want only good things for him, Miss Jones. Louisa would have, too. Since her death, he's become more... intractable. I might even say prideful. Or perhaps I just mean set in his ways."

Priscilla didn't know what the man was trying to get at, so she held her peace.

"I think you could be of great benefit to him. If you can find your patience."

"He's a mighty challenge just to be around. Don't know if I've got that much patience."

"Bea could use a woman's influence."

Here, Priscilla huffed a heavy sigh. "Don't know how much help I can be there, either. I know more about tracking deer in the woods than I do about raising a teenage girl."

"I would say what you did behind Madam Orr's today was a useful start. And that's putting it mildly."

"Y'all shouldn't go making so much out of it. They was both drunk."

"Why did you tell Bea the captain saved you?"

"Lots of reasons." Priscilla tried to sort out a few for the lieutenant. "She's got to have pride in her pa. A girl's father —well, we should think the sun rises and sets on them. They should be our heroes."

"And."

"Reckon his men oughta respect him, too."

"Oh, well, we do. Captain Corbett is well-liked, admired, and respected, but the story of how you singlehandedly took to task those ruffians is already circulating in the fort."

"Oh, that's a shame. Didn't want to take nothing from him."

"You may need to explain things to Bea. If she hears the other story—"

"I will be sure to."

They tromped up on the front porch of the captain's house and the lieutenant opened the door for her. "Well, Miss Jones, it has been quite interesting getting to know you."

CHAPTER 6

"Bea?" Priscilla called out.

"I'm in the kitchen."

Priscilla followed the voice and found the girl pouring a huge kettle of hot water into a copper sitz tub. On the stove, wisps of steam rose from a second, large kettle. "It'll be another few minutes. I usually like three kettles of water before I dip. You have time to unpack and bring down your robe or...whatever you might have for loungewear."

"Loungewear? Don't reckon I have any of that. I don't lounge."

Bea chuckled and shook her head. "You are more than I can figure out, Miss Jones."

"Why don't we do away with the formal names. Can't you call me Priscilla?"

"Priscilla. I'd like to thank you for what you did today." The girl swallowed like she was choking down her pride. "I —I was very frightened. And then I was frightened for you. My da got there just in time?"

A half-smile twisted on Priscilla's mouth. "Just in time. Rumors have a way of twisting things. You just remember he was a hero. Now, all I have in my satchel is two dresses, a few pairs of wool socks, one shift, and some long johns. Oh, and my Bible."

Bea blinked. "You've no corset or camisole or petticoat?"

"Nope. Are those lounge clothes?"

"Oh, dear." Bea replaced the kettle on the stove and used the potholders to grab and pour the second one. "I suppose I could get what you need from my mother's things."

"Oh, now, I wouldn't want you to do that. Not your mother's belongings."

Bea poured the water in silence. When the container was empty, she set it back on the stove. "There's the soap." She pointed at a cake sitting on the lip of the tub. She draped one of the potholders beside it. "You can use that for a washcloth. And this…" She pulled a bottle from the cabinet with a fancy, flowered label on it. "Shampoo direct from France. My grandda got it for me for my birthday. It will make your hair smell like a field of roses."

"Oh." This thought enticed Priscilla and she took the bottle for a whiff. "My, that smells prettier than honeysuckle in July."

Bea smiled at her, a bittersweet expression written in her pained brow. After a moment, she nodded. "I think my mother wouldn't mind at all."

SKYLER APPROACHED his home near the end of a row of clapboard houses built for officers. The general's house on the right was empty but waiting for his return. Nate's house was on the left. Skyler strode down the broad space between them, headed for the privy out back. Shared by all three households, it was rarely in use at the same time. As he emerged into his backyard, motion on his left caught his eye and he stopped as suddenly as if he'd walked into a brick wall.

A woman was hunkered down at the back door. A *naked* woman. Skyler blinked, unable to comprehend the vision. Water glistened on her tight, round backside, the swell of a breast flashed—

Alarm bells rang in his brain and he stepped back around the house. Out of sight.

Like a meteor show, probabilities shot through his brain all at once. A robber. A wild animal.

Miss Jones.

He nearly smacked his forehead. His house guest, was it? He peered around the corner. She was talking to someone, most likely Bea, and peering in through the glass, arms and legs crossed strategically.

Skyler didn't linger. Almost amused, now that he'd reminded himself no one was likely to see the scandalous situation, he hurried around to the front of the house, let himself in quietly, and barged into the kitchen.

THE DEEPER BEA dug into her mother's trunks, the more the flood of memories whirled around her. Before she knew it, her father's bedroom was covered with dresses, shoes, and framed photos...and at least an hour had passed.

With a gasp, she dashed downstairs to check on Priscilla and found the tub empty, her leather clothing draped over the back of a chair. Befuddled as to where the woman could have gone, Bea nearly jumped out of her skin when someone rapped firmly on the back door's glass window. She whirled and saw the top half of Priscilla's head, her green eyes as round as the harvest moon.

"The door's locked. Let me in." She ducked down out of sight.

Her bewilderment growing, Bea rushed over to open the door. The knob turned, but the door was stuck. "Just a moment. It sticks sometimes." Bea tugged again. And then again, even harder. "Oh, no. What are you doing out there?" And then it struck Bea that Priscilla was— "Are you naked?"

"Yes, I'm nekked," she whispered harshly, "as a jaybird. I just stepped out quick-like to see what was a scratchin' at the door and the breeze blew it shut."

"Oh, good Lord. Well, here, help me. You push and I'll tug."

"My backside is to the breeze. Let's make this snappy."

"Yes, yes." Bea grabbed hold of the doorknob with both hands. "On three. One, two—"

"My wee lass, I'm home."

Bea spun, putting her back to the door and blocking as much of the glass as she could. Da strode into the kitchen, dropping his hat onto the table. "Door stuck again?" he asked, moving toward her, hand out to help.

"Yes—no," she squeaked. "No, it's not stuck. Um..." She turned her head a little so her voice would carry to Priscilla. "I'm looking for Darby. My cat. He's at the front door now."

Da's eyebrows dove into the sinister expression of doubt. "I know who Darby is. Are ye all right?"

"Yes, would you go let him in?"

Her father looked at the empty tub and then back to Bea, the suspicion growing in his eyes. "Where is Miss Jones?"

Bea's mind went blank. She couldn't think of a single excuse. She shook her head, praying for something, but all that came out was the truth. "She is locked outside. The door is stuck."

"Oh, well, let me—" He reached for the knob and Bea swatted his hand back.

"She's naked."

The pure shock on Da's face would have made her laugh had she not known what would follow it. And in a flash, his expression flushed with fury. "What in the Sam Hill is she doing outside naked?" He pushed his daughter aside and laid hold of the doorknob, but stopped. "Miss Jones?"

"Y—yes?"

"I will avert my eyes, but get in this house this instant."

"Open the blasted door then!"

Da snatched the door open with a screech of wood. He turned his head and shut his eyes, and Priscilla lunged past him, almost slipping on a puddle of water on the floor. Bea grabbed her hand and whisked her upstairs. As they were lunging up the steps, Da's laughter—deep, robust, and filled with the most humor Bea had heard in months—echoed through the house and followed the two girls upstairs.

CHAPTER 7

"How in the world did you go about getting yourself stuck outside?"

Priscilla winced as the girl behind her pulled the corset ridiculously tight. "I heard somethin' scratching at the door. I stepped out—a little far, I reckon—and a mean gust of wind snatched the door right out of my soapy hand. Does this thing have to be this tight?"

"Yes, it does. Otherwise there is no point to it. Exhale one last time."

It might BE my last time. Priscilla did as she was told and the corset constricted a little more, like a rat snake squeezing its prey to death. "There." Bea smacked her on the shoulder. "How's that?"

"Oh, Lord, I feel like I can't move, much less breathe."

"Oh, that's fine. Now, we have to hurry. Da is most surely waiting on dinner. Let's see to your hair."

"Here, I'll just braid it quick-like."

"Brush it first."

Bea handed her the one from the dresser and Priscilla

marveled at the number of bristles. "My, that's fine. I only have a comb."

"The brush is much better for your scalp." Bea sat down on the bed and shook her head, as if Priscilla mystified her. "Is there some reason your da raised you like a boy? Didn't he want a daughter?"

"My ma died when I was young. Pa did the best he could and we figured out pretty quick I liked the forest and huntin' and fishin' a whole lot more than the kitchen. It was only there in the last few years of his life that..." That Priscilla had seen regret.

"That what?"

"I think maybe he regretted a little how I turned out." She swept her hair to one shoulder and began braiding it. "One of the last things he asked me to do was wear a dress once in a while."

"Well, he would certainly be pleased today. Look at you." Bea guided Priscilla to a long mirror standing in the corner.

Priscilla nearly gasped. It had been years since she'd seen her face so clearly, without splotches where the silver was coming off her mirror. And she'd never seen her whole body. She turned this way and that, enchanted by the way the green of her dress seemed to make her eyes almost... glow. And the crown of golden hair was blonder than she remembered, the braid longer than she'd realized, reaching her waist.

If she could only breathe.

"All right, we'd best get to putting something on the table. I'm sure Da is starving."

"Why do you reckon he was laughing? Was he laughing at me?"

Bea bunched her face into a tight little expression of serious contemplation. "I think maybe he was laughing at the both of us, and I have to say, I liked it. He hasn't sounded that happy in a long time."

"Guess I'm glad I could make him laugh, then. For your sake." Priscilla had enjoyed the sound of it as well, despite thinking it was aimed at her. The captain had a warm, rich laugh that was velvety, deep...even comforting. He had an edge to his tongue, however, that she wouldn't mind dulling with a hammer.

Oh, Lord, give me patience.

SKYLER'S LAUGHTER died as the girls disappeared upstairs and images of Miss Jones's slender, shapely body with its glistening, alluring curves returned to batter his mind. "Blast it," he muttered and tried to shake off the picture. He'd seen a naked woman before. He could objectively appreciate that Miss Jones had a fine shape and then move on from the incident. He was not a man ruled by base emotions.

He lifted a pot lid on the stove and glared at its emptiness. *What have these two been doing, if there is no dinner?* Hungry and annoyed over being so, he picked up a bright red apple and cleaned it on his sleeve. He wouldn't mind a bath himself—only, the kitchen might not be the best place to leave the tub anymore.

He took a bite of the fruit and pondered the females in his home. One growing into a woman, the other—well, he didn't rightly know what to do with or think of her. But she'd put Bea's safety above her own and he wouldn't forget it. He took a few more bites of the apple and then strode to the stairs.

"Ladies, might the lord of the home expect dinner sometime this evening?"

"I'm sorry, Da," Bea called. "That's my fault. I lost track of time. But we'll whip up something. Give us just a moment more."

Skyler grunted. He was hungry *now*. He supposed he could slip next door and see if his first officer's housekeeper had done *her* duty in the kitchen. *Lost track of time indeed...*

The soft rustle of cloth interrupted his mental complaining and drew his eyes to the top of the stairs.

For a moment, he stood dumbfounded. Skyler found it impossible to reconcile the lovely, curvaceous woman in an emerald-green dress floating down toward him with the leather-clad hellion in britches holding a knife to a man's throat. A long, golden braid hung down her shoulder, and he thought oddly of Rapunzel, and of loosening her hair. He could almost feel it between his fingers.

Miss Jones smiled at him and he literally blinked to clear his vision and his thoughts. Bea appeared over the woman's shoulder and grinned. "She cleans up rather nice, don't you think, Da?"

He frowned and stepped back. "Aye. Now, what about dinner?" Without waiting for an answer, he strode to his small library. "Call me when it's ready." He slammed the door behind him.

AN HOUR LATER, Priscilla and Bea set dinner on the table. Mashed potatoes, turnip greens, some sliced country ham, and a red-eye gravy that was a new dish to Bea, filled delicate bowls and platters. It didn't look like much, but there was also a pie still in the oven.

Priscilla had always cooked more than this just for her pa. She could usually eat more than this, too, but this blasted corset strangled the appetite right out of her. Made her feel a little faint, truth be told. *Probably just hungry,* she thought. "Well, Captain Corbett could either have a bigger meal later or a smaller meal sooner. Reckon he'll be satisfied with sooner?"

Bea set a basket of biscuits off to the side. "No. He's never happy with anything anymore, but at least he won't starve."

"For not having anything ready, I say we did pretty good."

The girl beamed. "Me, too. I'll get him."

Priscilla sat down, dreading the moment when the man would enter the room. He set her on edge to begin with, but being caught in her birthday suit, dang, if that didn't beat all. She didn't recall ever having been so embarrassed. His poor manners didn't make it any better.

A moment later, father and daughter entered the room. Priscilla watched with admiration as he pulled a chair out for Bea and situated her. Then he took his place at the head of the table and unfurled his napkin into his lap. "What did ye finally prepare?"

"Ham," Bea said, passing the platter to her father. "And Priscilla gave me the recipe—"

"Priscilla?" For a moment, he looked lost. "Oh, yes." He nodded at Priscilla as he took the ham. "Miss Jones. Of course."

Priscilla didn't know if she should be offended he'd so easily dismissed her name from his mind or grateful. She decided to be grateful...or at least try. Her pride stung enough from this rude man.

As they passed the food around, she wondered at the array of silverware Bea had laid out. Back home, she and Pa had never used anything but a fork, a spoon, and, if the meal called for it, their pocketknives.

She figured after the captain said the blessing, she'd hold

back a minute and see which of the two forks they grabbed first. To her surprise, the captain picked up the fork closest to his plate and shoveled in the first bite without grace. Then she remembered Bea's warning about the man's feud with the Lord.

She lowered her head, glanced quickly at the two of them, then said a soft, low prayer. The table quieted and she knew they were watching her. She finished in a hurry and grabbed the same fork the captain had picked up.

"There's no need to say thanks at this table," he said somberly, cutting into his ham.

"Maybe not for you," Priscilla replied, trying to keep her tone gentle while expressing her determination to keep on with the habit. The comment earned her a dark look from him.

The conversation flagged for a moment, but Bea tried to prop it up. "I guess I didn't need to bring out all the flatware, seeing as how we don't have a salad, Da. We do have dessert, though. There's a—"

"Pie," Priscilla squeaked, jumping to her feet. "The pie. I 'bout forgot it." She whirled and disappeared into the kitchen.

SKYLER LOOKED TWICE to make sure he'd seen what he thought he'd seen. As Priscilla had lunged for the kitchen, he'd caught a flash of...feet. *Bare* feet. Unbelieving, he kept his gaze on her hem when she returned carrying a pie. Sure enough, her toes peeked out from beneath her simple dress.

Dear God, my father has sent me a mannerless, brainless wildcat from the Blue Ridge Highlands. This willnae stand.

Miss Jones set the steaming pie down on a crocheted place mat and settled into her seat once more. She paused, took a small breath—in a pained way, he thought—and then smiled at Bea. "Smells good. I love a warm apple pie." She frowned and touched her stomach, as if it troubled her.

Skyler bounced his fork in his hand, searching for a kinder way to express his thoughts, but to no avail. He was too jumbled. No. The word offended him. He was not jumbled by this woman. He was annoyed with her. As he was annoyed with his father for causing this ridiculous situation.

He argued once more that he was not *jumbled*—even as the images of a naked Miss Jones darted in and out of his brain. He stabbed a piece of ham. "In this house, madame, we do not run about like savages," he said too sharply. "Clothes are required at dinner, as are shoes."

Priscilla had a bite of mashed potatoes at her lips, but paused when she apparently realized the comment was aimed at her. Her lips tightened into a vague sneer, but she blushed at the same instant. Skyler scolded himself for yet again being less than polite. He'd not had to work on manners for so long that they had escaped him.

"My feet offend you?" she asked, setting down her fork. "Back home, on summer evenings after dinner, we'd wander out to the front yard and walk through the cool grass barefoot. It's a mighty nice feeling on a warm night."

Skyler was completely baffled as to her point. "Bully for ya enjoyin' yer country-bumpkin rituals. Here in—"

Miss Jones whipped her head around to Skyler. "Who you callin' a country-bumpkin, you silly, preening rooster?"

For a moment, Skyler was at a loss for words.

The woman had actually sassed back. Again. And insulted him. He didn't know how much more of the wench and her back hills ways he could take. "My house, my rules," he barked, slamming his fist down on the table. "Ye'll wear shoes, or ye'll not eat at my table."

Miss Jones's face darkened to beet red. Skyler knew he'd both embarrassed and infuriated her. He thought for a moment she was reaching for her knife, when Bea intervened.

"Da," his daughter said softly, "Priscilla has had a different upbringing than us, is all. She'll learn our ways. But we have to teach her. *I'll* teach her."

Before he could respond, Priscilla slowly rose to her feet. "I'll learn your ways soon as you learn some manners." She picked up the small, ornately engraved, unnecessary salad fork from the table and pointed it at him. "Fancy plates and silly rules is window dressing for a man who ain't got any better manners than a snarling badger. In fact, I know..." She shook her head and started again. "I know fellas back home with...with..."

The woman swayed on her feet. When her eyes rolled back, Skyler realized what was happening. As Miss Jones fainted, he dove to her side, barely managing to fold her into his arms without bringing the tablecloth with him. "Here now—" he snapped foolishly.

"Da!" Bea lunged to her feet and pointed. "It's her corset," she cried. "Cut the corset."

Skyler immediately laid Miss Jones on the floor. With unabashed violence, he ripped open her dress, which buttoned down the front, and then swiped the steak knife from his plate. He gathered her up again, slid the knife around to her back, and sliced the blade up through the lacing. Feeling the pressure loosen, he tossed the knife, grabbed the front of the garment, and snatched it off her body.

Tossing it away without any thought, he clutched the woman's chin and shook her. "Miss Jones, ye must take a breath." When she didn't respond, he shook her whole body with greater force. "Miss Jones, breathe, woman, breathe."

Suddenly, she inhaled, choked, and clawed at the air as if she were swimming to the surface of a deep pond. Skyler, surprised by the level of relief he felt, turned her face to him. "It's all right, lass. Yer fine now. Just breathe."

Glimmering, jade eyes, wide with panic and still focused on an unseen terror, finally came to rest on Skyler. Almost immediately, she relaxed. The fear left her gaze. He thought she almost smiled at him. She certainly was a pretty thing with the most flawless skin he'd ever seen, and he couldn't help letting his fingers touch her rosy cheek.

"Miss Jones, are ye all right?"

She blinked, frowned, then comprehension dawned and she closed her eyes. "Dear Lord, I fainted like a candle on the stove."

Skyler took stock of the moment, the woman in his arms, the pleasant way she fit, and his daughter hovering over them. The pleasant feeling turned to something like panic and he rose, bringing Miss Jones with him. "Here now, see if ye can stand." Eager in an odd way to be rid of her, he set her at arm's length. She swayed, he clutched her shoulders, but she shook her head and waved him off.

"I'm all right. All right." She pulled the back of her hand across her forehead. "Just let me sit down and have a sip of water."

"Here." Bea hurried around to the other side of the chair and poured a glass. Skyler helped the woman ease into her seat. She took the water and downed two big gulps. She nodded and licked her lips. Skyler breathed a little easier.

"Damnable things," he muttered, taking his seat. "Corsets. A bit of feminine trickery, in my opinion."

Miss Jones took a deep, invigorating breath. "I'm inclined to agree."

Bea returned to her seat and ogled Miss Jones. "You're

sure you're all right?" Her gaze dropped repeatedly to the woman's torn dress.

"I reckon so." She looked down, saw the condition of her clothing, and pulled the pieces together. "Ain't never fell-out like that before. I can do without it. And the corset." She gasped softly here at something in the corner and they followed her gaze. "The corset," she repeated. The garment, its strings cut in two, lay in a heap at the foot of the buffet. "I'm so sorry, Bea."

The apology bewildered Skyler. "'Tis only underwear."

"It was Mother's," Bea said softly.

Skyler felt the cut, the slice of the jarring words keen and deep. His chest constricting, he refused to sit here and deal with the pain in front of the women. Slowly, he rose to his feet, not even sure where he was going. "Bea, I'll...uh, eat later. Keep a plate warm for me, if ye would."

He drifted from the kitchen, feeling like a ghost. One trapped in the past.

CHAPTER 8

"It's been an eventful day."

Nate's voice pulled Skyler's gaze from the sunset-washed prairie and distant Rockies. "Aye." Plucking his pipe from his mouth, he nodded at his friend ambling up the walkway. "An understatement."

"What do you think of her?"

Images flashed through his mind and he cleared his throat. What was the matter with him? "She's an opinionated lass, stubborn and sassy."

"Hmmm." Nate's brow dipped as he reached the porch and leaned on the rail. "I'm not sure if you're complimenting her or insulting her."

"Clearly not a compliment. No mon in his right mind would want a woman with those traits, lad." Skyler shook his head. "A handful of trouble, that one."

"Well, you may have to keep your hand full for a while."

Again, images—intriguing, dangerous—erupted in his mind, and he pinched his brow, trying to force them into the dark. "Ye've news?"

"The patrol caught up with One-Who-Cries and his warriors at Devil's Back. He had a hostage. A White girl. Shots were exchanged, but no casualties. They lost them in the canyons."

Skyler cursed. "That Indian is a menace. We've got to figure a way to put him down like the rabid cur he is."

"Yes, sir, I don't disagree. He's elusive, though. He and his band, some of the finest riders I've ever seen."

"Then we'll send our best after him," he snarled, determined not to let this marauding murderer take any more lives.

"Yes, sir." Nate hooked his thumbs in his belt and kicked a toy mouse the cat terrorized. "Sir...Skyler...the stagecoach is closing down the Southern route till further notice. Your...houseguest might be here a while."

Skyler sighed heavily. Of all the blasted inconveniences... Strangely, the thought of her in his arms came back to him and he scolded himself immediately for the train of thought. He'd been too long without the ministrations of a woman. He was, after all, not dead. And Miss Jones was not unpleasant to look at.

But she was mouthy, he reminded himself. Mouthy, uncouth, uneducated.

On the other hand, the woman had proven herself useful in multiple ways. Perhaps she might keep Bea busy. Not to mention safe. But what kind of influence might she exert on the girl? If he ever saw his own daughter in britches—
"Orders," he said aloud. "I'll give her and Bea clear instructions on their duties and my expectations."

"Orders?"

"Aye. Orders. I'll spell them out. It'll be fine. If I'm to be stuck with the lass, she'll learn some manners and serve a purpose."

"Orders," Nate repeated, a little flatly, as if debating this plan.

"Ye've a problem?"

"No. It's just that I wonder if you understand they're women and not soldiers."

"With proper leadership, there is very little difference."

CHAPTER 9

"Order. Discipline. Without them, there is chaos."

Priscilla wiggled uncomfortably in the dining room chair as Captain Corbett paced back and forth, droning on and on about a *regulated* life. An organized life birthed efficiency. Priscilla couldn't figure what he was getting at and wished he'd just come right out and say it.

In the meantime, she studied him, because coming to in his arms had been about the nicest thing she'd ever felt. She'd gone all warm-and-gooey inside, like a fresh apple fritter, and she wanted to know what could be the cause. Maybe it was his army uniform. He sure cut a dashing figure in it, the dark blue blazer a flattering fit on his broad shoulders and narrow waist. It made him even more imposing and authoritative.

Priscilla acknowledged it was difficult not to be cowed by him, and this befuddled her. No one had ever cowed Priscilla Jones. Those that had tried never tried again.

Captain Corbett's dark honey hair, moving gently with every duck and nod of his head, brought her halfway back to his speech and she caught something about *womanly arts*. Then the lighter strands of honey glinted with the morning light and she wondered how soft it must be. She actually wiggled her fingers with the desire to touch it.

Every now and then, he'd say a word that took her a second to translate. Once she'd figured out a few things like *woomon*, *cood*, *wood*, and *dinnae*, and the cadence with which he spoke, his speech didn't leave her as confused. But there were still mysteries.

He passed his stern gaze back and forth over her and Bea as he talked, the intensity in it drying her throat. Finally, he stopped and faced them. "In short, what I'm saying is we'll run this house as good as, if not better than, the fort. I will give you a list of chores and tasks. You'll have them completed every day before I return for supper. Is that understood?"

Chores? Sure, she knew how to do chores, and she nodded her understanding. As did Bea.

"In addition, Miss Jones, I have some specific rules ye will follow. Going forward, ye willnae wear your buckskins anymore. Do ye ken?"

She frowned, trying to sort through his gibberish and find the point. No buckskins? The menfolk around here couldn't seem to keep their eyes in their heads when a gal in britches walked by, so she nodded. Not to be hemmed in, however, she added, "I won't wear them around here."

"By God, woman, I say you don't wear them anywhere. They're not decent."

Fury streaked through her veins at the order and she nearly jumped to her feet. It wasn't her fault menfolk couldn't control their brains, but a pleading glance from Bea convinced Priscilla to swallow this pill. Perhaps it would be safer for the girl when they were out, as well. She consoled herself with that thought and nodded. "Fine."

"Da, Miss Jones has very few dresses and fewer...undergarments. I'll have to take her shopping."

"Fine. Whatever it takes, make her presentable."

Priscilla would not be forced into another corset if her life depended on it, but Bea dang near wiggled with excitement at the idea of shopping. So, once more, Priscilla gave in. "All right."

"Second, if ye must ride a horse, ye'll do so sidesaddle."

"What?" Priscilla yelped, coming to her feet. This was pushing it too far. "Why don't you just hog-tie me and throw me over the saddle."

Scowling, Captain Corbett leaned toward her. "Dinnae tempt me." Their glares locked, the temperature in the room rising, he added slowly, grimly, "A lady rides sidesaddle."

"Don't you think you can do it?" Bea asked.

Priscilla huffed in disgust. The rule was stupid, and Bea's challenge was an obvious ploy. "I can ride a horse six ways to Sunday. With a saddle or without. But hanging off the side—you just don't have enough control."

All the times she'd galloped through the mountain laurel and up the rocky slopes of the Blue Ridge with Cherokee renegades or hungry cougars on her heels rocketed through her mind. God forbid, if she'd been riding sidesaddle, most of the races would have wound up with her as the loser.

"While ye're here, ye will ride sidesaddle." His tone said he'd brook no cussedness on her part. The stubborn set of his jaw warned Priscilla to tread lightly.

"Fine." She was coming to loathe the word.

"And as for you, lass..." He turned his attention to his daughter. "There will be no more assisting any of my soldiers with chores or following them about unless Miss Jones is by your side."

Bea gasped and then set her jaw right back at her father,

crossing her arms over her chest. "I don't need her to watch over me. I'm fourteen years old."

"Aye. That is precisely why she'll be by yer side when any event or activity involves my men, especially young Private Willoughby."

Bea blushed three shades of red and glared at her pa. She was madder than a wet hen and Priscilla liked it. *Rules not so funny now, are they?*

"Do ye ken my meaning, girl?" He shifted to Priscilla. "Do ye?"

Priscilla nodded. "I'm her shadow."

"Closer."

Bea huffed again, but the captain ignored it and continued. "Last, Bea, ye'll teach our little bobcat here some womanly arts."

Priscilla grimaced. "You mean like needlepoint and drawing?" Two things she considered colossal wastes of time.

"Aye, Bea is good at those. Perhaps the piano, too."

Bea slumped but didn't argue. Feeling a little defeated herself, Priscilla sat down again. Sidesaddle. Needlepoint.

Oh, Pa, what have you done to me?

Captain Corbett grinned like a man who had just stolen the election for county sheriff. "Fine, then, ladies. I'll see ye at supper. Oh, and Nate will be joining us this evening." He dipped his head in goodbye and strode from the house.

PRISCILLA WAS PRETTY DISPIRITED OVER ALL this, but it seemed she had no choice. She looked over at Bea. Bea looked at her and shrugged. "Guess we could start with shopping."

"I guess...but I won't have your pa pay for my dresses. I got money."

"You do?"

"Pa had Doc Owens help me sell the farm. The money... he called it my dowry."

"Oh, that's so sweet." The girl clasped her hands and laid them over her heart. "Your da put so much thought into this."

"Yeah, I reckon he did."

"Owens?" Bea tilted her head. "That's Nate's last name. Wouldn't it be funny if your Doc Owens and he were related?"

Priscilla scratched her head. "Would explain a few things, too. I knew Doc had a son, but he moved to Ocoee after the boy was already in the military. I never met him." *But Pa did.*

Priscilla slid her gaze to the window that looked out on the house next door. Did this Lieutenant Owens know something about this arrangement? Was he the reason Pa had shipped her here to Colorado?

Good thing he's coming to dinner, 'cause I intend to ask him.

"BUT YOU *HAVE* to wear the corset," Bea said to the dressing room curtain. "You need the—" She lowered her voice. "The support."

"I need air more."

Admittedly, Bea had felt a bit foolish putting a corset on Priscilla yesterday. She had a lovely figure. No doubt, the men in the fort would think her waist was perfect. Besides, she was muscle from the top of her head to the soles of her feet. Her stomach looked harder than an actual corset.

Maybe Bea just needed to accept the female on the other side of the curtain was a different beast.

"I'll wear the dang shift," Priscilla muttered, her words muffled and surrounded by the sounds of material shifting. "I'll wear the bloomers. I'll even wear this petticoat." She popped her head out between the curtains. "But I will not wear the corset, and that's that." She nodded perfunctorily and disappeared back into the changing room.

"Very well. I won't fight you on it. I like wearing mine. It makes me feel very feminine and grown up." She wouldn't mention how constricting it was or that she had nearly fainted once herself. "Are you ready for the dress?"

Priscilla's hand shot out through the curtain. "Yes, please."

Bea passed the first one in. A simple day dress of light blue spattered with brighter cornflowers. It would be love—

Priscilla's hand appeared again, still holding the dress. "Nope. I need 'em to button in the front."

"I'll help—"

"Nope. I'm not gonna be beholding to somebody just to get dressed."

"But I'll be arou—"

"You might not be."

Bea took the dress and handed Priscilla the other one she'd been holding. A dress done in yellow with little pink bows down the front. Thus far, her personal favorite.

"Oh, Lord," Priscilla whined. "I'll never keep this one clean."

"I'll get you an apron for it."

"All right. All right."

"You know, this is a small shop. They don't have tons of dresses from which to choose."

"Surely there's a few more out there that button up the front."

Mrs. McCloskey, an older woman, white-haired and as jolly as she was round, walked up. "Can I help you find anything else, Bea?"

"Yes, ma'am, if you please. Anything that buttons up the front."

"I have a few. I'll bring them all over."

CHAPTER 10

BEA HAD TO LAUGH AT PRISCILLA'S REACTION TO THE RED dress done in red and black plaid. She simply fell in love with it and insisted on wearing it out of the store, though it was rather Christmassy. Mrs. McCloskey wrapped everything else up in brown paper packages tied up with string.

They had their hands full carrying the load down the street, and Bea nearly dropped hers, but Private Willoughby ran up and caught them with a gleaming smile. "Goodness, ladies, allow me." He took two packages from Bea and three from Priscilla.

Bea felt her cheeks warm and she smiled broadly at the young man. He was tall and handsome, tanned from the sun, and just the most perfect thing she'd ever seen. His uniform was dusty, though, as if he'd been on a long ride.

"Thank you, Mr. Willoughby. Oh, this is Miss Priscilla Jones. She'll be staying with us until the stage lines open up again."

"Oh." He nodded and smiled, white teeth glowing against his sun-kissed face. "Miss Jones, gee, I sure heard an interesting story about you."

"You mean about how Captain Corbett saved me from those ruffians?"

A dip appeared in the boy's brow. "Uh, well, that's not exactly the way—"

"Stories get all twisted up and confused the more they're told, but that's the gist of what happened, ain't it, Bea?"

"Oh, yes, Da was magnificent the way he leaped on his horse and took off, followed by Sergeant Bonhoeffer using no tack at all."

"Yeah, the Sarge is one good-riding horseman...so, where are we taking these?"

"Back to our house." Bea blinked, letting her lashes flutter. "I hope it's not inconvenient for you."

"Not at all."

The three of them strolled on, Bea wishing that Private Willoughby was beside her rather than in the middle.

"How is your horse doing?" Bea asked.

"Thank you for the suggestion about his feed, Miss Bea. Sergeant Beale said he's prone to gain weight, so I'm to exercise him an extra twenty minutes a day, as well."

"I had a horse like that," Priscilla said. "Had to work to keep him away from clover, otherwise he'd blow up like an expectant mare."

The group laughed at the image.

"So, where are you from, Miss Jones?" Private Willoughby asked.

"Ocoee, Tennessee."

"I'm from Memphis."

"Oh, I went there once with my pa. I was just a young'un and don't remember anything except the Mississippi."

"Yeah, it's memorable all right."

"I've traveled the Mississippi twice," Bea interjected. "On a paddle wheeler. It was lovely."

"Yeah, nice way to travel," Mr. Willoughby answered.

"So, Miss Jones…uh, Ocoee. That's in the mountains, isn't it?"

Bea frowned. Why was he so interested in Priscilla?

"God's country," the woman answered. "I sure miss the smell of honeysuckle and mountain laurel, but I could get used to it around here."

"It's different, for sure. We'll have to go for a ride up in the mountains—all of us," he added, smiling at Bea. "They're something here. Taller than anything back East."

"Hmmm." Priscilla nodded. "Reckon I'd like to see mountains bigger than the Blue Ridge. Can't even imagine such."

"Oh, some of the mountains here stay topped with snow all summer. Why, look there…"

As they stepped off the boardwalk to cross an alley, he pointed off into the distance. The Rockies rose up from behind a row of cabins, a little hazy, but blue and shimmering. Snow did, indeed, cover the tops of several.

"I noticed them earlier," Priscilla said, studying the view.

"That big, tall one, that's Pike's Peak. I've heard it's nearly fourteen thousand feet high."

Priscilla smacked him on the arm. "You're joshin'."

"No, ma'am. That's what I'm saying. The Rockies are monsters."

"My lands," she whispered, sounding awed.

The trio resumed their trek, passing the sentries at the gate. Bea didn't see Sergeant Bonhoeffer this morning. She did see all the men watching Priscilla, who seemed oblivious to their stares. She was busy gazing off at the mountains.

As they walked on, Da waved from the top of the north wall. At first he smiled, but it faded quickly when he noted Mr. Willoughby's presence. "Where have ye been, Bea?"

"We went shopping, Da, to get Miss Jones some things. Private Willoughby happened by and offered to help."

"How mighty polite of ye, Private. Hurry back to yer duties when ye've delivered the ladies."

"Yes, sir." The boy snapped a smart salute. "Right away."

Da started to turn away, paused for just a second to note Miss Jones, then continued quickly on his walk—his afternoon inspection.

"You heard the man, Miss Bea. Miss Jones. I'd best hurry."

Bea huffed softly to herself as Private Willoughby rushed them back to the house. If Da hadn't interfered, they could have had a nicer, slower walk...

Instead, Private Willoughby delivered the packages to the porch, tipped his hat, and ran off to get back to his duties. Bea bit her lip and watched him go. She was a little disappointed. They hadn't had much time to speak and he'd directed more questions at Priscilla than her.

Of course, that could be because she was new to the fort.

"Nice fella," Priscilla said, coming to stand beside her. "But you heard what your pa said."

"I heard."

It didn't mean she'd obey.

"Well, come on." Priscilla hugged her packages a little tighter and reached for the ones Private Willoughby had dropped. "We've got to put these things away and get to your pa's list of chores."

THE REST of the day passed in a whirlwind of chores and Priscilla was glad. If she stayed busy, she was less inclined to ponder the troublesome, little thoughts that buzzed in her brain like honey bees. She and Bea dusted and swept the house, then put two chickens in the oven to bake. After that, they sat on the back stoop and peeled a mess of potatoes for dinner.

"Aw gratin, you say?" Priscilla shook her head. "No, I ain't never had it. Sounds good, though. I like cheese."

"We'll prepare them and then put them in the oven with the pie."

The comment didn't need a response. Priscilla tossed her clean potatoes into the large bowl between them and pulled another one from the sack.

"How old do you think Private Willoughby is?" Bea asked carefully.

The boy filled the girl's brain. Priscilla would have chuckled...except for the fact that a man now invaded her own thoughts, along with a million other things. "Oh, he looks to be eighteen or so."

"I'm fourteen. Do you think he's too old for me?"

"Yes."

The girl sucked in an offended gasp and her mouth turned down in despair. "Why do you say that?"

Maybe Priscilla was no scholar when it came to love, but she knew when a man looked at a girl and saw a girl—not a woman. How to say that without offending Bea, though? "Well, maybe what I mean is you ain't growed enough yet to get his attention."

Bea opened her mouth as if to argue, then shut it suddenly. Her brow creased and she appeared to be thinking fiercely hard on something. "What do you mean?"

"When you talk to him, does he look you in the eye, good and deep, or touch you real light like?"

She slouched a little. "No. And he's never touched me."

"Your pa said not to follow the men around or help with their chores. Was you doing that to Willoughby?"

"Maybe."

"And when you did, did he slow down and let you help, or did he keep on with things?"

Her shoulders drooped a little more. "No. He just kept moving and talking to me over his shoulder." She brightened suddenly. "But he does have a pet name for me."

"Oh?"

"He calls me...kiddo." The joy went out of her and she slouched again. "He does think of me as just a kid. A little girl."

And that was exactly what Priscilla had observed earlier. The private did seem like a nice young man, but he looked right through Bea. Worse, he'd given Priscilla a couple of careful, appreciative glances, though he was younger than her by a good three or four years, she guessed. She was glad he had not made any flirtatious remarks in front of the girl.

"What can I do?" Bea sounded heartbroken.

"All I know is grow up some. See if he notices then."

"But that means waiting, and I don't want to wait for him to notice me."

"One day, just out of the blue, I bet he'll look at you and see right away how pretty you are."

"When, Priscilla, when?" Bea pleaded with blue eyes full of hope and youth.

"In the Lord's time."

Again, the girl exhaled with sadness and frustration. She reached into the burlap bag at their feet and came back empty-handed. "That's all the potatoes."

"Why don't you go on in and get these to boiling. I'll chop a little wood. The pile's low and I'll get it built back up lickety-split."

～

As Priscilla picked up the axe left in the stump, the bees began buzzing in her brain again. *Where do I go if this doesn't work out, Lord? Reckon there's anything I can do to get the captain to like me? I sure wish there was a creek nearby so I could do a little fishing...*

That thought stopped the swing of the axe and she looked around. The officers' houses were inside the fort. Fifty or so yards off, just beyond the privy, a twenty-foot-high wall of logs blocked her view of the mountains. Blocked her view of everything. She felt as hemmed in as a sow in a pen.

Maybe things will get better, she told herself, taking another swing with the axe. *Please, Lord, may they get better.*

While Captain Corbett and Lieutenant Owens enjoyed pre-dinner cigars on the front porch, Priscilla and Bea finished getting the meal on the table. As they bustled about, Priscilla caught snippets of the men's conversation in somber, troubled tones. Something of a serious nature was going on with the Indians in the area.

"...more attacks expected..."

"They might lay low..."

"Sharpen the cavalry..."

"...Scaring or killing our scouts."

When she returned to the table to set down the pie, she was surprised to hear her name and couldn't resist a little more intentional eavesdropping.

"The woman is a comedy of errors," the captain lamented, raising Priscilla's hackles and cutting her to the quick.

"Maybe, but it sounds as if she was exactly what Bea needed."

"Aye, at that moment. 'Tis true."

"She and Bea do seem to get along. Have you given any thought to her as a possible wife—?"

"Priscilla, did you put on any coffee?"

Dang it. Bea's question interrupted the captain's answer. Though, Priscilla didn't need to have it spelled out on a chalkboard. The captain didn't cotton to her. She was both relieved and disappointed. Which was foolish and double-minded of her. *Just like a woman not to know her own mind*, Pa would have said.

"Coffee? Uh, no, I hadn't made it that far." She placed the pie on the table. "I'll do it right now."

OVER DINNER, she could tell the men were attempting to talk about the Indian trouble in veiled tones. Lieutenant Owens cut into his elk steak and shook his head. "Second scout this month to…go missing. We're running low."

"Aye, start sending them in threes. Safety in numbers."

Priscilla had been involved with some of the Indian trouble back home. Even fought a brave who tried to take her scalp. "Are the renegades here as ferocious as the Cherokee?"

Captain Corbett gave her a stern look. "Cherokee are like toddlers compared to the Cheyenne."

"Tell the settlers killed along the Oconaluftee that."

The captain huffed over her challenge. "All Indians are dangerous killers."

"No, that ain't true, either."

"Woman," he snapped at her, "cease your contrary conversation."

"I'm not trying to be contrary, Captain. I've got friends back home that are Cherokee. God-fearing folks, they are.

And citizens of these United States, rightfully recognized as such in '68."

"Miss Jones, the East has been settled. The Indians have assimilated. Out here, we're still tying up loose ends."

"That's my point. You've got a few rascals to deal with, sure, but most of them have come to terms with things. Don't go callin' them all killers."

"Ye've not fought them as I have. They're a murderous, treacherous bunch."

"It's been my experience, Captain, most of the Indians want peace. But they want and deserve not to have their land stolen from them."

"Are ye sayin' we should step aside and let the wild ones murder our people?"

"'Course not. Some of these young bucks, well, some of them you just can't reason with."

"Exactly."

"But you can't judge a whole nation of people based on just the crazy ones."

"The crazy ones," the captain repeated slowly, "are the ones I must protect our people from. Forgive me if I'm not able to spot the friendly ones from the crazy ones at a distance. I am, as a matter of fact, in favor of Indian sovereignty, but my opinion is neither here nor there. I have my duty."

"Miss Jones," the lieutenant cut in, as if heading off the conflict at the table. "You have familiarity with the Indian problem?"

"Like I said, I've got friends back home who are good people. And I've had my run-ins with a few who weren't so good. We've got renegades, too." She flicked her own glance at Captain Corbett, then continued with the lieutenant. "Speaking of home, I just realized today your last name is Owens, same as the doctor's back in Ocoee."

The lieutenant's hand froze in its pursuit of his next bite. He cleared his throat and stabbed a bit of potato. Captain Corbett had paused ever so slightly, as well, and Priscilla did not miss the glance the men at the table exchanged.

"The doctor is my father, Miss Jones. I was in Ocoee this Christmas past."

"Well, that sure explains a lot. I guess you had something to do with me finding my way here, then." She had wanted to say *being shipped off*, but held back from any ugliness. She did not know this man's part in her fate and would let the story unwind, if there was one.

"I suppose, to be honest, my comments about Captain Corbett in front of your father must have spurred some of this."

"No good deed goes unpunished," the captain grumbled, slicing off a piece of steak.

Priscilla almost grumbled right back about the captain's mood and manners, but forced herself to stay quiet. She was not the contrary one at the table. Though she was getting very tired of deflecting his fiery arrows.

"I met your father, Miss Jones, one afternoon just after New Year's. My father took him a bottle of whiskey. I tagged along. You were out with a hunting party."

"A hunting party?" Captain Corbett repeated. "I don't know why that surprises me. Clearly, it shouldn't."

But he said it like Priscilla had gone down to the local saloon. The insult was the last straw. She waited for him to look up at her. When he did, she thought past his pretty blue eyes and determined not to be ashamed or embarrassed of her upbringing.

"Somebody had to hunt for my pa. He wasn't able in the last few years." She leaned in a little closer, her anger boiling. "And I'm a pretty dang good scout, too. If you're losing yours, you should get better ones." She jumped to her feet and tossed her napkin down. "Sending 'em by threes is just gonna lose 'em faster. Bea, I'll be back to help with the dishes."

With that, Priscilla stormed from the room. She'd had all she could take of the man's pompous, prideful vanity. He was just a loud, crowing rooster who didn't know when to hush up.

IN THE STUNNED silence left by Priscilla's abrupt departure, Skyler froze with the fork near his mouth, then finished the bite. He did not look at Nate or Bea until he reached for his water. Bea was a portrait of frustration with her little, pinched brow. Nate regarded him with only a slightly more patient look of frustration.

Well, Skyler McTavish Corbett would not be cowed or contradicted by a highland tart. "I'll not be argued with by a woman in my own home. She, and you, young lady"—he pointed his fork at his daughter—"will keep your opinions to yerselves."

"If she has experience with Indians," Nate began gently, "she may have something of value to say."

"Thus far, what I've seen is a woman with no manners, no education, and no boundaries for spinning yarns."

Nate's brow rose. "You don't believe her?"

"Nay."

"But what about those men—"

"She herself said they were drunk."

"She stood up to them to protect me," Bea interjected, then flagged a little. "But she did say you got there just in time."

"Aye, she did." Why did she do that?

"But she—" Nate squashed whatever he started to say,

considered things for a moment, then tried again. "My father told me that Mr. Jones's daughter was something of a bobcat. He'd patched up some of the men she'd *tangled with*, as the locals put it."

"Ye must call them rumors and innuendo," Skyler said. If word got out that the woman in his house was a better warrior than most of his soldiers—no, there would be hell to pay for everyone involved if the men took that as fact. He'd already met with Sergeant Bonhoeffer and pointed out that neither he nor Skyler had actually seen her fight the men. Hence, this spreading of Calamity Jane rumors needed to cease.

Bonhoeffer had agreed, saying he felt a bit foolish for falling for the girl's big talk. Somehow she'd simply gotten the jump on a pair of drunken fools.

"Da, regardless of what you think of Priscilla, you haven't been nice to her since she stepped into this house. You're not being much of an officer or a gentleman."

Nate dropped his head, no doubt to hide a smile, as Skyler froze. Bea could play him like a violin. Assailing his honor was a low blow and she knew it. Worse, he would have to agree with his daughter. He bounced his fork in his fingers for a moment, then set it down in his plate with a crystal-clear clink sound. "Ye might be in the right on that. I'm a big enough mon to admit it."

"Bea," Nate said, rising and picking up his empty plate. "Why don't I help you with the dishes, so your father can go offer an apology."

"I'll do no such thing," Skyler snapped, greatly annoyed at being maneuvered into this.

"You should have seen the way she gazed off at the mountains today." Bea's tone picked up a sticky, sweet, melancholy edge. "She called her home God's country. She's away from everything and everyone who mattered to her, Da. How can you treat her so?"

Her pleading eyes and Nate's gaze that challenged him to be a better man won out. Sighing, Skyler pushed back from the table, drummed his fingers for a moment, then rose and went to the mantle. "I believe I'll have another smoke." He plucked a Cuban cigar from the humidor, sniffed it, and nodded. "Outside."

NIGHT HAD FALLEN. The chill in the air was pleasant. The last ray of dying light faded behind the black outline of the mountains in the distance. A few feet from the end of Skyler's walkway, the pair of grounds-patrolmen passed by, making a circuit of the parade ground first and then the rest of the fort.

As he struck a match on his porch post and lit his cigar, the weak light illuminated a tiny figure. Curled up on his porch swing, she hugged her knees in close, as if the world was a mountain lion about to pounce.

He exhaled smoke softly, quietly. He supposed he had been a bit of a cad. The poor girl was a pawn in a mean-spirited game. The letter he had just mailed to his father clearly expressed Skyler's disdain for the joke and forbade his father from ever involving an innocent in any of his future pranks.

How could the man have been so callous?

"That Willoughby boy," Miss Jones said quietly, coolly, "You ain't got nothing to worry about. Yet."

Skyler appreciated her speaking first. Perhaps his apology—when he got 'round to it—would come easier. "Really? How are ye so sure?"

"The way he was looking at her. Sort of like a growed dog looking at a puppy."

He rolled the image around in his brain for a moment. "He still sees her as a child?"

"For now. But it won't last long. She's hankering to be a woman, and everything is starting to fall into place, so to speak."

Skyler cleared his throat. He was not comfortable talking about his daughter becoming a woman. Or the men in the fort noticing. Neither did he want the men to grasp what an unusual woman Miss Jones was.

Why was that?

Partly, he did not want to be a laughingstock. She was uncouth, rough-spoken, *countrified*, his father, the lord, would have said. Furthermore, she was fast, lean and strong, and he had no doubt the girl could wrestle and probably beat most of the men in the fort. He'd felt the strength in her when she'd leaped like a deer into the saddle with him, seen too much of her shapely, compelling curves when she'd been locked out of the house.

But more so, he knew his men. They could count the number of women in Rose Creek on their fingers and toes. They would be falling all over themselves to court Miss Jones once more of them got a look at her in a dress. And this probability rankled Skyler, though he couldn't say why.

Sucking on the cigar, he leaned back on the rail, positioning himself between the post and a healthy fern Bea nurtured faithfully. From the swing, Priscilla looked at him and he was struck by the comeliness of her face in the dim light. High cheekbones, big eyes, full lips accented beautifully with the play of the shadows.

"And it'll happen overnight."

He blinked, confused for a moment. Oh, yes, Bea. "How is it ye know so much about raising a daughter?"

"I ain't so smart. It's just the way of things. Kittens grow into cats. Lambs grow into sheep. Fathers grow old and die...and daughters..." She trailed off, sounding forlorn and lonely, but her words were laced with wisdom. "Daughters grow into women," she added. "That's life."

To some extent, Skyler thought perhaps he had misjudged Miss Jones—then he observed her carefully slide her bare feet beneath her dress—and recanted on the notion.

Still, he'd come on a mission and he did not ever shirk his duty. "Miss Jones, possibly I've been a bit harsh with ye. I hope ye'll forgive me. This situation is not to the liking of either of us, but there's nothing we can do about it for now. So, I'll endeavor to be more..." He stumbled here. Soft-spoken? More willing to accept her opinions? He didn't want to lie. "Aware of yer feelings."

To his surprise, she half-chuckled, half-snorted in what sounded like derision.

"Is that funny?"

"Back home, there's a Cherokee preacher. He talks a lot about the Word of God and the Word of Man. God says what he means and means what he says. Man plays games with words."

"I fail to see yer point." As he failed to keep the irritation from his voice.

"You said you're sorry, but you didn't say you'd change anything."

For an instant, Skyler wished his officers were as perceptive as this girl. Then he hissed out a little breath, feeling as if he'd been caught with his pants down. "I'll try to work on my boorish manners, yer ladyship. Good night."

CHAPTER 11

"O Romeo, Romeo! Wherefore art thou Romeo?

"Deny thy father and refuse thy name.

"Or, if thou wilt not, be but sworn my love,

"And I'll no longer be a Capulet."

Bea looked up from the book in her lap and tilted her head at Priscilla, puzzled by the grimace on the woman's face. "Does your stomach hurt?"

"My brain hurts. This fella Shakespeare talks like he's from another century."

"He is. This story is over three hundred years old."

Priscilla huffed. "No wonder. All right, so what's going on there? She's asking him to give up his name?"

"And if he won't, she'll give up being a Capulet."

Priscilla bit down on her bottom lip and shook her head. "This ain't going to end well. Feuding families are an ugly thing to behold."

"Families can be vicious." Bea closed the book. They had chores yet to do and a few more genteel arts to attempt before it was time to start dinner. "Would you like to work on your needlepoint or knitting skills today?"

A dark, disgusted look clouded Priscilla's face once again. "My fingers are sore from needlepoint yesterday. Reckon I'll try the knitting again. Seems a touch less dangerous."

Bea stifled a chuckle as curiosity about Priscilla washed over her. She pulled out the sack with their knitting needles and yarn and passed out the items. "Tell me about your home and what things you did there for fun."

"Fun?" Priscilla took her needles, green yarn, and her lumpy, irregular potholder wrapped around them. "Fun," she repeated as she awkwardly positioned the tools and yarn in her hands. "I fished a lot from a fast, wide creek. A mile or so from the cabin, there was a lake. Big, blue, and in the mornings, it was calm and flat as a mirror. My canoe..." She studied the stitches she'd just made with a pensive dip in her brow.

"Loosen your grip," Bea reminded her. "Relax your fingers."

Priscilla did as commanded and continued. "My canoe used to slice across that water faster than a flick. And it was quiet. It was like another world out there, with the mist clinging to the mountains, sometimes not a sound. Not even a bird. It was something to behold."

"It sounds lovely."

"And sometimes in the summer, I'd climb to the top of our mountain and sit and watch the fireflies come out." Her eyes frosted over and she was lost in her memories, Bea could tell.

"Were you lonely? Or did you have a beau?"

The question seemed to snatch Priscilla back abruptly. She sniffed and focused intently on her knitting. Bea didn't push. Perhaps she had overstepped.

After a minute, though, Priscilla shook her head. "I was outside more than I was in. Why, if I wasn't hunting with

Pa, I was throwing my knives, or racing my horse through the meadows. I was real good at all that. At first, the boys seemed to like it, but..."

"But?"

"I was better at almost everything. Boys don't take to losing. Even the one or two fellas who gave me butterflies— well, I-I just didn't want to act like a weak, eyelash-batting, mushy-brained girl to catch a fella. At first, Pa said, 'Good for you, girl. Show 'em what a Jones is made of.'"

"And then?"

"In the last couple of years, he told me to go to the dances in town, wear a dress to church, quit scaring the boys away, but I—I didn't know how not to scare 'em by then."

Bea thought about things for a moment, wishing she were older and wiser and had something insightful to say. Like the way Priscilla had pointed out Private Willoughby didn't see Bea as a woman yet. It struck her then that Priscilla had the same problem, only it wasn't the men. Priscilla didn't see herself as a woman.

"Did you ever go to any of the dances?"

"I started out a couple of times but somehow wound up sitting on Buzzard's Roost, watching the sun set over the lake. Gee, it was a beautiful sight. Besides, I don't know how to dance."

What a strange girl, Bea mused again. *She can throw a knife, but she can't dance.* "Can you *really* throw a knife?"

"I can part your hair with one."

"Truly?"

"Truly. But I wouldn't. It might make your pa mad."

Still, Bea had to see this. "Come with me."

～

A FEW MINUTES LATER, they were standing behind the house. Bea had propped a potato on the chopping block using a small stone while Priscilla retrieved a knife from her room. "Can you hit that?" she asked as the woman emerged from the house.

"Sure."

To Bea's amazement, Priscilla only drew within ten or so feet of the spud. "Throwing down at an angle is a little harder, but I think I got it." She flipped the bone-handled knife around so the blade was in her fingers and then swiftly launched it, spearing the potato dead-on. It rolled to the ground, the knife sticking out both sides.

Bea's mouth fell open. "Dear Lord, you can throw a knife." And Priscilla had done it as naturally and as easily as Bea took a breath.

"Told you I could." With a jaunty step, Priscilla hurried over and pulled the knife free. "Want me to do it again?"

Bea was astonished and intrigued. "Yes—no. Yes. I mean, yes, but can you teach me?"

Priscilla fluttered her lips and narrowed her eyes at Bea. "I'll teach you to throw a knife…if you won't make me do any more needlepoint."

Bea laughed and rushed over to Priscilla, her hand out. "I'll do one better."

"What's that?"

"I'll teach you to dance."

"I have kind of hankered to learn. All right."

"It's a deal."

Grinning big and bright, Priscilla shook Bea's hand with a bone-squeezing grip.

∼

"AND WHAT DID ye two ladies get into today?"

Priscilla exchanged a knowing glance with Bea across the dinner table.

"Knitting," the girl said, passing fried squash over to Priscilla.

"And Shakespoint," Priscilla added. "Bea reads real well."

"Shakespoint?" Captain Corbett blinked and looked at Bea.

"She means Shakespeare. I'm reading Romeo and Juliet to her."

The captain chuckled in a dismissive way that again brought up feelings in Priscilla that she wasn't used to. He made her feel sort of giddy when he was around, but at the same time, he made her feel lower than a snake's belly.

"Shakespeare," she repeated, vowing mentally to never forget it.

"Ye should get out my Robert Burns and read something better than that Englishman."

Bea rolled her eyes. "Da thinks Mr. Burns is the end-all, be-all to literature."

"What does he write?"

"Poetry." Bea wrinkled up her nose. "It's awful. Maudlin and melodramatic."

Captain Corbett pointed his steak knife at his daughter. "Now, none of that. He's the official bard of Scotland."

Priscilla and Bea both focused on the knife in his hand, read each other's thoughts, and burst out with giggles. They had a secret, and it was a fine one.

The captain's face tinged pink and his lips thinned. "Ladies, your chortling at the table isnae ladylike. I'll appreciate it if ye stop. Or let me in on the joke."

"No joke, Da, just..." She faded off, scratched her chin, then smiled at her father. "Why don't you read a little of Mr. Burns to us this evening? On the porch, before the light is gone."

He raised a brow at his daughter. "And what is it ye're up to?"

"I'm not up to anything. I just thought Priscilla might enjoy it."

Priscilla held her face still. Listening to someone read poetry wasn't exactly the same as riding her old gelding Charlie Boy across a green mountain pasture. Those days were gone, though, and she reckoned she'd best get a handle on things. "That sounds...fine."

NOT LONG AFTER, she and Bea went outside and sat down on the swing. Priscilla gazed longingly at the short, struggling grass on the parade ground. It wasn't fescue, but she thought it would still feel pretty nice beneath her feet. She sure would be happy to kick off these lace-up boots that made her feet ache and find out. They were so confining.

"Do ye have a request, Bea?" Captain Corbett asked, appearing in the doorway. He held a book in one hand, a pipe in the other, and smoke curled around his head. In the waning light, it set up an odd glow around him, almost magical, Priscilla thought.

"Red, Red Rose."

"Aye." He crossed the porch and leaned on the rail, stuck the pipe back in his mouth, and flipped through the book. "One of my favorites," he said, teeth clenching the device. "Here it is."

Bea wiggled around, getting more comfortable. Priscilla wondered just how long this poem reading was going to take but settled a little deeper on the swing, too.

"My love is like a red, red rose that's newly sprung in June..."

Priscilla turned her head, pleasantly taken aback by the captain's deep, husky voice.

"O, my love is like the melody that's sweetly played in tune."

It was hypnotic. So soft on her ears, she could almost feel it. His words fell like a caress.

"So fair art thou, my bonnie lass." He looked up, and their eyes met. "So deep in love am I." He snatched his gaze back to the page. "And I will love thee still, my dear, till a' the seas gang dry." His voice softened a touch more, his cadence slowed. "Till a' the seas gang dry, my dear, and the rocks melt wi' the sun, I will love thee still, my dear—"

"The flan." Bea rose from the swing. "Please keep reading, Da. I'll be right back."

He frowned at her interruption and cleared his throat. "Would ye like me to continue, Miss Jones?"

"Oh, yes." She would never admit the pleasurable feeling she got from his voice, but she honestly thought she could sit here all night and listen to it. His pipe had gone out and he laid it on the small table near the door. Tugging on his coat, almost as if he were a touch nervous, he returned to the book, but stood a little taller, a little straighter. "I will love thee still, my dear, while the sands o' life shall run."

Priscilla closed her eyes and let his voice glide over her like a fine piece of silk.

"And fare thee well, my only love. And fare thee weel awhile! And I will come again, my love, though it were ten thousand mile…"

He finished the last words softly, like a man reading a prayer, not a poem. Priscilla opened her eyes and found him looking at her. "If it were not for the slight smile on yer face, I would fear I had put you to sleep."

"No, not at all. Those were some pretty words, and you sure read well, too."

"Well, that's kind of ye." He glanced around them, rocked on his heels. "Would ye...like to hear another?"

"I would." And another. And another. It vexed Priscilla that this man could be so rude, and yet she found herself wanting to stay in his presence, listening to him, content as a kitten in a sunny window, his voice as gentle as a butterfly's wings.

"Very well." He flipped a few pages, found another poem, and started to read when the crunch of gravel made him turn. Lieutenant Owens jogged toward him, holding a piece of paper up.

"Dispatch, Skyler. From the general."

Disappointed at the interruption, Priscilla hauled herself off the swing. "I'll see if Bea needs help and bring y'all some coffee, if you'd like."

"That would be lovely, Miss Jones," Lieutenant Owens said. "I could use a cup."

"Aye, thank ye, Miss Jones."

"Coming right up."

SKYLER WATCHED Priscilla disappear inside as Nate stepped up and handed him the dispatch. He took it absently, his gaze on her slim figure, the blonde hair spilling down her back. He noted and appreciated the girl's beauty with half his mind, but the other half pondered the expression of contentment on her face as he'd read to her. As if she'd never heard poetry before and it had moved her.

If only she were more—

Fingers snapped in his face and he whipped his head back around to Nate, who was grinning like a man with a glorious secret. "The dispatch. It's from the general. You remember him."

Embarrassed—and angry over being so—Skyler glared at him, opened the note with sharp movements, and read the words.

They made him want to bang his head against the post.

"Lovely," he muttered and read them again to make sure he had all the details. "The general will be back from Washington in two weeks. We're not only to make sure his house is ready, but he'd like to host a gala, as he is bringing dignitaries."

Nate rolled his eyes. "Dignitaries. Politicians. I think I'll go fight Indians."

"Aye." Skyler glanced back inside the house. *Good Lord, what will the general think of Miss Jones?*

"How are you and your houseguest getting along? Any romance on the horizon?" Nate wiggled his eyebrows.

Skyler almost growled. "I dinnae appreciate yer sense of humor."

"I saw you looking, Skyler. And she's nice to look at."

"Aye, but that upbringing of hers..." He dragged a hand over his chin, hesitant to explain his concerns, but Nate should be aware. "She's an embarrassment, lad."

"Her grammar is a little rough—"

"Nae, it's more than her manners. I think she could tangle with and beat half the men in this fort."

"I thought you didn't believe the stories about her."

"I was trying to downplay them, to keep the men's morale up and their curiosity about her tamped down. Those two drunkards that she bested, however, won't shut their gobs."

"I don't think I understand what's bothering you."

Skyler continued, annoyed that Nate couldn't grasp the problem. "These Calamity Jane rumors will only intrigue the men. They'll be knocking down the door to visit with her, and she's in my house."

"And?"

"'Tis beneath me to watch over the virtue of a countrified waif," Skyler snapped. Why was this so hard for Nate?

"Beneath you?" The lieutenant scratched his nose and paced a few feet down the porch, head down as if he were pondering the uncomfortable situation. "I don't know how to address your offended sensibilities—"

"*My* offended sensibilities?"

"Your title is showing, Lord Corbett."

"I'm no lord, I'm only his son."

Nate grunted. "Potato. Potahtoe."

"What's that?" The comment baffled Skyler.

"Nothing." Nate waved his hand. "If you've no matrimonial interest in the woman, see if she'll stay as your housekeeper and nanny. Though, I would suggest never use the word in front of Bea."

"Aye."

"And as far as the men, well, you can't keep the girl locked up. You're right, tongues are wagging about her."

"Aye, I know."

"The best you can do is demand the utmost gentlemanly conduct from anyone who comes calling. If you're not going to put a claim on the girl then—"

"I can discourage them outright."

Nate frowned. "As I was about to say, if you're not going to put a claim on the girl, she's a right to see whomever she wishes. I'm not sure it's your place to interfere."

"She's under my roof," he barked. "I've no choice. My house, my rules."

Nate dropped a hand on his friend's shoulder and laughed. "If I didn't know better, I'd say you're trying to keep men away from her...for...your own interest."

"I've no interest in her whatsoever. And, as I said, I dinnae appreciate your poor humor."

"It was just a thought." He smirked and Skyler was tempted to wipe the expression off his face but moved on to a more serious matter.

"Speaking of troublesome women, I've made the decision to send Bea to a girl's school in the fall."

Nate sucked in a breath. "That won't make her happy. She loves it here with you."

"I know, but I should have sent her sooner."

Nate shoved his hands in his pockets and jangled the change in his pocket. "I suppose you have your reasons, and I wouldn't presume to tell you what's best for your daughter. It will break her heart, though."

And mine, too. Something Skyler did not wish to think about at the moment.

~

"SHE'S AN EMBARRASSMENT, LAD."

Priscilla jerked to a stop at the door, nearly spilling the two cups of coffee on the tray. Of course, she knew who embarrassed the lordly Captain Corbett. Since they were discussing her, she felt wholly justified in further eavesdropping, even though everything coming out of the captain's mouth made her want to spit nails.

...countrified maiden...

...'tis beneath me to watch over...

...my house, my rules...

The frosting on the cake for Priscilla was Captain Corbett's audacity to think it was his place to keep her out of trouble. Would he, indeed, lock her up in this house to hide her from curious eyes? Time for the two of them to come to an understanding.

Almost past being weak-kneed over his pretty blue eyes and velvety voice, Priscilla let herself outside and glared at

Captain Corbett. He could hurt her feelings with his uppity attitudes, but nobody took Priscilla's freedom. Nobody. "We'd best talk."

"Um, I think I'll have my coffee inside." Lieutenant Owens plucked his mug from the tray. "Good luck, Captain. Thank you, Miss Jones." He skedaddled into the house like a gun-shy dog.

Captain Corbett calmly lifted his cup from the tray but paused with it an inch from the surface. "Or perhaps I should leave this so ye don't hit me with the tray."

"Won't stop me, either way."

He *harrumphed* and took the coffee. "I take it ye heard some of our conversation?"

"Yep."

"And ye're offended."

"Aw, now, why would I be offended? Just 'cause your Lordship thinks I'm an embarrassment." She lowered the tray and poked him in the chest. "So, let's just get a few things out of the way right now. I'll be your housekeeper till such time as I can leave. I'll take care of things around here, and that includes Bea, but you will not tell me where I can go, when I can go, or who I can talk to. We got an understanding, Captain?"

"God above," he thundered, nearly spilling his coffee, "if ye're not the sassiest wench I've ever come across."

She jabbed him in the chest again, harder. "And don't you forget it."

CHAPTER 12

Skyler was surprised by the quiet house. Home for a midday break to grab another one of the scrumptious biscuits from breakfast, he slapped some ham on one and then went in search of his daughter. And perhaps Miss Jones was about...

Peeking into the parlor, he was surprised to find two large sketchbooks open and lying on the coffee table, charcoal pencils scattered about. One page showed a young girl in a fancy dress with a large bustle. Bea loved drawing gowns. Her work was a touch amateurish, but her scale was getting better.

The other sketch...he picked it up, impressed. A lovely landscape of rolling hills, with mountains in the background and pine boughs and laurel in the foreground. It gave the impression of peering through the trees, pulling the observer into the image. *Bea should do more landscapes*, he thought.

"Do you like it?" she asked from behind him.

"Aye. I was just thinking ye should do more of this kind."

"Priscilla sketched it."

Skyler didn't think he could be any more surprised if he found out the woman was related to DaVinci. "Did she now?" Miss Jones was full of surprises.

"She took to drawing as if she'd done it all her life. A few lessons and she turns out something like that."

"She's a gifted artist, then," he admitted grudgingly.

"She said that's the view from Buzzard's Roost, her family's mountain."

Skyler studied the fine details of blossoming rhododendrons, a few birds perched here and there on pine branches, the rolling hills that led up to distant mountains, all in shades of gray, yet he could so clearly imagine the colors. It reminded him much of his youth in Scotland and his trips into the Highlands. "It's lovely. Miss Jones has unexpected skills."

"You've no idea, Da, how skilled she is." Bea chuckled and Skyler clearly detected the sound of someone keeping a secret.

He did not, however, have the time or inclination to pursue such trivialities. "Good. Then perhaps she'll have dinner for the general well in hand before the gala."

"Da..." Bea slithered around to face him. "About the gala." Sugar dripped from her tongue as she straightened Skyler's lapel. "May I attend this year?"

"No."

She huffed and stomped her foot, instantly furious. "Why not? I'm fourteen. I've—"

"Aye. When ye're sixteen, ye may attend with an escort of my choosing."

His daughter's face scrunched in anger, her cheeks bloomed red...and then suddenly, it all melted away, leaving behind an angelic expression. "What if I had an escort now who would watch me like a hawk?"

Skyler saw immediately the trap into which he'd stepped. "Miss Jones, I assume ye mean."

"Yes. And I bet she'd love to go to the gala, as well."

He had time to figure a way out of this. Over a week. He need not deal with it now. "I'll think about it." He took a bite of his ham biscuit and sauntered out the door.

SKYLER AMBLED back to his office, nibbling on his biscuit and returning salutes as he passed his men. He found himself studying their faces more closely. Most of them were pimply-faced, gangly, eager to fight anything that moved, blindly living like death wouldn't come for them at any second. These would be the first to call on Miss Jones. They would see her as a challenge. She would see them for the boys they were.

No, his cadre of officers was more fitting for the girl— and yet, they weren't right for her, either. Nate was a good man, and he and Miss Jones had struck up something of a friendship, but Skyler couldn't see that working—

Abruptly, he stopped walking, astonished at the direction of his thoughts. The wench had wormed her way into his mind much, much too often. This would not do. He had a fort to run and settlers to protect. There was only one way to get his mind back on his business.

Go out with a patrol.

NATE BOISTEROUSLY ARGUED against Skyler's plan, to the point Skyler almost became angry with him. He turned his back on his friend and swung up into his saddle. "It's been a while, Nate. The men need to see me doing the things I ask them to do."

Nate surrendered, raising his hands. "All right. I'll pray it's an uneventful day."

"I'm sure it will be. If it's not, however, I pray it's One-Who-Cries who is the event."

≈

SKYLER SHOULD HAVE BEEN MORE careful with his words.

He hunkered down behind a rock as bullets ricocheted from the canyon walls. They'd stumbled across the band of renegades a day's ride out from the fort in the El Chico Canyon—because their three scouts had deserted in the night.

The sun sat directly above him and the patrol of fifty men, beating on them with merciless heat. Skyler's head swam from the temperature and sulfuric smell of gun smoke in the air. He touched his side, slick with blood, and acknowledged perhaps the bullet was also to blame for his lightheadedness.

He aimed at movement. The bullet whizzed past the target, zinging musically off the rocks. *Bea*, he thought. *I didn't tell ye today I love ye.*

His men kept up the volley until Skyler thought he detected a decline in the return fire. "Sergeant Bonhoeffer," he yelled to the man behind a rock some dozen or so feet away.

"Yes, Captain," he replied smartly and fired at a target.

"They're dividing."

"Yes, sir, I believe they are."

"Send ten men to the rear to guard the horses."

Bonhoeffer bellowed the order and ten men moved past

Skyler so low to the ground it was a wonder they weren't on their bellies.

The firing went on another several minutes until Skyler was sure the volume had decreased at least by two-thirds. No attempt had been made on the horses. He glanced back at the men behind him and was forced to blink away his double-vision. The renegades had been slipping away, a few men at a time.

Skyler cursed. He should have seen this.

Woozy. If I just had a little water...I could think better.

"Captain, I think they're slipping out on us," Bonhoeffer yelled. "Shall we give chase, sir?"

The revolver slipped from Skyler's hands and bounced down the steep, rocky incline in front of him. He touched his side. *I'm shot,* he meant to say aloud, yet the words wouldn't go past his lips. A fog of darkness rose up from the canyon floor before him and he let it envelop him in a gentle embrace...

CHAPTER 13

"It ain't so bad." Priscilla spoke calmly and wiped the blood away from the captain's side. "I think I can..." She pressed gently around the wound. "Yeah, I can feel it. It ain't deep." She looked up at Bea and Lieutenant Owens on the other side of the bed, both of whom were white as midnight ghosts. "The bleeding has slowed a considerable amount, but we need to get that bullet out. How much longer 'fore the doc gets here?"

"I don't know," Nate said, grimacing. "He's in town somewhere. I'm sure we'll find him. Not much longer, I assume, but I just don't know."

She dabbed at the wound again, the rivulet of blood steady but not a gusher. "Well, I can take it out. There's no need to wait."

Nate put his hand out. "Are you sure you should do that?"

"Reckon I'd better."

"Don't worry, Nate." Bea squeezed his arm. "I've seen what she can do with a knife."

"Bea, there's a small leather satchel in my room. Sitting on my dresser. Would you fetch it for me?"

"Certainly." The girl was off like a shot.

"Miss Jones," Nate pressed, "you're offering to perform surgery on my commanding officer...and my friend."

She looked up and saw the concern evident in his pained, brown eyes. "Don't worry, lieutenant, it ain't deep. He's lost a lot of blood, though, 'cause of the wild ride back here. I need to get him sewed up."

Nate nodded and took a step back from the bed. "Very well."

NOT UNTIL EVERYONE had left the room did Bea allow herself to cry. She clutched her father's hand, sleeping peacefully now, and prayed. "He'll wake up, Father. I know You won't take him, too."

And she believed that.

Doc Bannon had come along at the time Priscilla was starting to sew. A bean pole of an older man, he'd leaned down close to her hand, frowned at her in passing, and examined the wound. Looking at her over the tops of his glasses, he'd eyed the needle and catgut in her hand. "You any good with those?"

She glanced at the wound. "I can do a little hole like that."

Doc motioned with his hand. "By all means, please continue."

He'd stayed close, nodding his approval as she sewed. With the last stitch, he grunted and straightened up. "Fine, fine. Impressive stitching, young lady. Not your first, by the looks of those sutures."

"I've sewed up a friend or two."

Doc drifted his fingers over the wound once more. "He'll probably come around in a few hours. I'll stick close to the fort for the next day or so in case you need me lickety-split. By the way, I'm Dr. Bannon." He offered his hand.

Priscilla took it and gave her hearty grip. "Priscilla Jones. Nice to know you."

Slight perspiration sparkling on his forehead, he pulled his glasses off and studied Priscilla for a moment. "Where are you from, Miss Jones?"

"Ocoee, Tennessee."

"Small place?"

"Barely a crossroads."

He chuckled. "Folks in those small communities learn to doctor themselves to survive."

"Reckon so."

He patted her on the shoulder. "Well done. Thank you."

Priscilla shrugged, looking sheepish. "I didn't do anything special."

Dr. Bannon's brow shot up. "Madame, you have no idea how few women would have done what you did. God bless you for your courage." Then the doctor looked at Bea. "Your father is going to be all right, in large part due to this young lady."

And then they had left, and, finally alone, Bea cried. She cried because she had to release the fear that had choked her into silence as she'd watched Priscilla work on her father. She cried because she was grateful to Priscilla for being so courageous. She cried because she was grateful that the Lord had sent them Priscilla.

Muffled voices in the hallway interrupted her tears. Sergeant Bonhoeffer and Nate inquired after her father. Priscilla and the doctor updated them, then all the voices faded away and Bea squeezed her father's hand tighter.

"Oh, Da, I'm sorry," she whispered. "I'll never sass you again."

"Promise?" His voice, weak, raspy, sent a shock wave through Bea's heart.

"Da?"

He opened his wonderful, magical blue eyes and gave his daughter a faltering smile. "What happened?"

"You were shot, but you're all right."

He seemed to mull over the information, then his forehead creased with worry. "Casualties?"

"Nothing that needed a doctor."

He started to move but winced and touched his side. "I've stitches?"

"Yes, but only five. Dr. Bannon said you'd be all right soon."

"Aye, I will. No wee bullet will keep me down."

Bea couldn't resist a little shock for her father, as well. "The doctor also said Priscilla did a wonderful job with your stitches."

"My stitch—ye mean, she—?"

"Yes. She had her own medical bag with instruments, catgut, even a little bottle of something that smelled like witch hazel."

Her father heaved a heavy sigh but didn't say anything else. Neither did she. She knew that look. Deep, smoldering, contemplative. Priscilla seemed to challenge everything her father believed about people.

And she thought that was a very good thing.

WHEN SKYLER THOUGHT of Miss Jones, the myriad images were so diametrically opposed to one another that he thought it possible his brain might hemorrhage. He'd seen her nearly nude, beautiful and glistening, hiding on his back step. He'd seen her clad in buckskin, fearlessly holding a knife to a man's throat. He'd seen her descend a set of stairs in a simple dress and, yet, look as beautiful as a princess.

He shook his head and took a puff of his pipe as he stared across the parade ground, silent and still in the final throes of sunset. Still, except for a soft summer breeze that moved the tops of the cottonwoods bordering it.

His side twinged, reminding him of her other skills. She could sew like a surgeon, fight like a man, and sketch like an artist. And all the men had heard the story of her surgery. Men of every lower caliber and quality would be sniffing around to court her. Coming to his door.

If only she had the grammar and more genteel qualities of someone of good breeding. Her poor grammar, rural background, and unusual skills made her introduction to society...impossible. He flinched when he thought about it. And the general was due literally in the next day or so.

Again, he thought of his father, staging this huge, painful joke. Skyler had mailed him a letter and spared no comments about Miss Jones or the prank orchestrated in such poor taste. He puffed on the pipe and considered the next steps, the best way to handle this.

Of course, he had only one option. Oddly, it didn't sit as well with him as he'd thought it would. Nonetheless, there was only one remotely acceptable way Miss Jones could stay under his roof: as his housekeeper. He would introduce her to the general and his party as such.

The station suited her.

And so it would be.

CHAPTER 14

SKYLER SIPPED A CUP OF COFFEE AND WATCHED AS MISS JONES cooked eggs and bacon for him. "Ye're handy in the kitchen. I've quite enjoyed yer biscuits."

"Ain't my favorite place to be, but I can manage."

Yes, no doubt she preferred running barefoot in the dewy grass like an Indian. He could have rolled his eyes but refrained. Her qualities were either endearing or maddening. If he were a different man, he would say endearing. As of now, they were maddening. "Miss Jones, before Bea comes down, I'd like to clarify our current arrangement."

"I sort of thought we had." She swung 'round with a pan of sizzling eggs and slid them on the plate in front of him.

"Well, yes, but I wanted to mention that the general and his guests will be in today. I'll expect a higher level of formality in…this." He motioned to the kitchen.

"Sure. I've done got a menu picked out. I think your guests will eat well."

"Fine, then."

Bea strode into the kitchen, yawning and stretching, her vibrant red hair controlled in a neat braid—similar to Miss

Jones's. There were worse women his daughter could mimic, but if he ever caught her wearing britches...

Bea delivered a sleepy kiss to the top of his head and joined him at the table. "Good morning, Da, Priscilla."

"Mornin'. Like some eggs?"

"Yes, please."

"Bea, the general will be joining us for dinner. Wear something nice."

"All right."

He finished his coffee and rose. "We'll be here around six. Good day, ladies."

They bid him goodbye and he trudged toward the front door, his mind on Miss Jones's apparent contentment with the current arrangement. Perhaps because it would be temporary and she focused on that.

He was reaching for the doorknob when he noted movement on his porch. A blue uniform. Curious, he stepped out to find Private Clark waiting, his kepi in his hands. The boy snapped to attention and saluted, his eyes round with shock.

Skyler returned the salute absently. "Mornin', lad. Is there a problem?"

"Uh, no, sir..." His gaze flitted to the door and he smacked the palm of his hand nervously with the hat. "I was just...just..."

"Aye?"

"Well, I was just wondering if Miss Jones might be headed into town or anything. I don't have to take my post till ten. I thought I might assist her."

Skyler dropped a fist on his hip, barely missing his stitches. "Miss Jones is busy. I'm sure there's something more useful ye can do than bandy about on my porch like a rooster. Off with ye."

"Uh…" Disappointment swirled on the boy's clean, soft, baby face.

Irritation crawled over Skyler like ants. "How old are ye, boy?"

"Eighteen, sir."

"And how's ye're hearing?"

"Fine, sir."

"Then ye're old enough to understand an order. Clearly, ye can hear one."

The boy sighed, nodded, saluted, then trudged off the way he'd come.

Skyler tapped his foot, the drumbeat of aggravation. Women. They scrambled every man's brains. Sighing in disgust, he stormed off the porch.

PRISCILLA STEPPED BACK a little and let Bea inhale the wonderful scents coming from the oven and the stove.

"For a girl who likes hunting and fishing better than cooking, you learn fast."

Priscilla picked up the spoon and stirred the savory-smelling sauce for the chicken. "I just like them better. Never said I couldn't do the other." She grabbed a potholder from the stove and opened the oven door. "Here, let's get these pies out."

Next, Bea showed Priscilla how to set the table and explained what each utensil was for. Though they wouldn't be using all of them, the table was set beautifully and everything glittered beneath the candlelight. Voices drifted in the front door and Bea straightened up. "The general. He makes me nervous. He jokes a lot, and sometimes he isn't joking, and I don't know how to talk to him."

"Ladies," the captain called from the parlor. "We've guests."

"Bring them in, Da. Dinner is ready."

A little nervous herself, Priscilla retreated to the buffet and clasped her hands in front of her. A group of four people entered with the captain. The big man in the uniform with a chest full of medals was no doubt the general. Tall, barrel-chested, his voice was as deep as his shoulders were wide. Two younger men followed him, wearing nicely tailored suits of black wool.

But on the general's arm hung a woman of breathtaking beauty and elegance. Dressed in a chocolate silk gown that matched her hair, she dripped with diamonds. They nestled in her hair, surrounded her throat, hung from her wrist. Her eyes, however, were what truly caught Priscilla's attention.

She'd accidentally cornered a mountain lion one summer when she'd been out tracking deer. Coming around a rock formation, she'd surprised the cat sniffing the entrance to a cave. In an instant, the animal had sized up Priscilla, defined her as an enemy, and lunged. Priscilla would never forget the cold, heartless look in the cat's eyes or those fangs and teeth coming at her.

Only her pa's fortunate timing and good aim had ended the matter.

Pa wasn't here now, and Priscilla saw that same cold expression in this woman's dark gaze.

The captain motioned to his daughter. "General, of course you know Bea."

"Of course. My, you've grown into a lovely young woman in just the last few months."

Bea blushed, giving the group a chuckle.

"The young lady beside her, General, is my housekeeper, Miss Jones."

"Oh, Miss Jones, I'm delighted to hear Skyler has taken on help. He certainly needs it. It's wonderful to meet you."

"You, too. Thank you."

"Miss Jones," the captain continued, "the lovely lady on his arm—a surprise to us all—is Miss Danielle Quartermaine, the daughter of Senator Quartermaine."

Cold, green eyes drifted over Priscilla. "Miss Jones, it's a pleasure."

"Yes." She nodded. "Nice to meet you."

The woman's lips twitched like something was funny and she covered her mouth with a gloved hand.

"And these two troublemakers," Captain Corbett finished, "Are her unruly brothers, Henry and Jack."

The young men greeted Priscilla with friendly smiles. "Miss Jones."

"Miss Jones, a pleasure."

Priscilla returned their warmth, but she could feel the unexpected daggers in Miss Quartermaine's gaze. As the group took their seats, all of them, Priscilla understood what was happening. The table was full. She was no longer a guest. She should have, of course, expected this. She saw now that the captain had tried to explain this earlier. Her embarrassment heated her cheeks.

"Da, we need a seat for Priscilla."

Captain Corbett shot Priscilla a troubled look. "Um…"

"I'll start bringing out the vittles. Y'all just enjoy." Holding a big smile, she hurried back into the kitchen. As the door closed, she heard Miss Quartermaine. "Oh, what a precious woman. That accent. Where did you find her? She's positively adorable."

Adorable? Priscilla didn't feel adorable. She felt frumpy and tossed aside.

Priscilla had plenty of experience waiting on men. The ones who formed the hunting parties back home often started the day at her and Pa's place. Feeding them was the neighborly thing to do, of course.

Cooking big batches of food and filling the plates of hungry folks was nothing new to her, and she took care of Captain Corbett's guests with a sweet smile and fast service. She took special care of Miss Quartermaine. Not out of kindness, Priscilla admitted—more for the reason you don't turn your back on a snake.

The girl batted her eyelashes at the captain, spoke to him more than anyone else at the table, laughed at his jokes, touched his arm every chance she got. Most annoying, however, was the way she looked right over Bea, like the girl wasn't there.

Priscilla gripped the edge of the sink and glared at the dishes. Or, rather, through them. The face of the catty Danielle Quartermaine rose before her. Pretty, petite, with rosy cheeks, a tiny waist—obviously the woman didn't mind a corset—brown hair piled high in no doubt the latest style. She sure made Priscilla feel frumpy and about as pretty as a piglet.

But standing here mewling like an angry calf wasn't getting the job done.

Before she tackled the dishes, Priscilla took one last sweep of the dining room table to make sure she hadn't forgotten anything. The table was clean, but the captain and his guests had retired to the porch. The heavy, sweet smell of tobacco smoke drifted through the open windows and tickled her nose.

Voices filtered through as well. The delicate, crystalline laughter of a woman hung in the air. Captain Corbett's voice was low and soft, almost soothing. Irritation burned a little brighter in Priscilla as she swiped up a forgotten coffee cup.

The man sure sounds like he's having a good time, she complained mentally. But drawn to the conversation, she paused, openly eavesdropping. After a few minutes, she deduced the general, Jack, and Henry were gone, the lieutenant was either oddly silent or missing, as was Bea. Priscilla heard only the captain and Miss Quartermaine. They seemed to be having a friendly, relaxed time.

If he can't see through that little hussy, he deserves her claws. She flinched. *I'm sorry, Lord. I didn't mean that.*

Determined to think of only the dishes, she dove into them with a vengeance.

But the captain and his guest on the porch invaded her thoughts with every breath. Every little ladylike chuckle or low rumble of the captain's laughter scorched her spirit.

"Tarnation, what's the matter with me?" she whispered, scrubbing a plate.

A moment later, she heard shuffling behind her but didn't turn. Captain Corbett's arm slipped in front of her, two empty mugs in his hand. "May I?" He motioned to the sink. Priscilla nodded and looked up as he slipped them into the water.

His face was only inches from hers. Blue eyes filled her world, her thoughts, took her breath for a second. His hand slowed and he held her gaze. He had fine, little lines that met at the corner of his eyes. Laugh lines, Pa had called them.

"I'm ready, Skyler."

He blinked, dropped the cups, and attended Miss Quartermaine. "Aye." He nodded. "I'd like to get my pipe. Give me a moment."

"Certainly."

Priscilla could feel the woman's eyes bore into her back as the captain exited to fetch his pipe. Priscilla considered turning but decided instead to ignore the woman. Miss Quartermaine was not inclined to return the favor, apparently.

"Where are you from, Miss Jones?"

"The mountains of Tennessee."

"Oh, that explains your delightful accent. It's so...rustic."

Priscilla knew the word. It was no compliment. She snuffed a sassy reply and kept to the dishes.

"Skyler tells me you have many unique...gifts. Among other things," she muttered, but Priscilla knew she was supposed to hear it. "And"—she started laughing—"he was regaling me with a story of you coming to dinner without shoes." Miss Quartermaine's voice sang with amusement. Every note drove Priscilla's spirits a little lower and a little lower.

"Reckon I'm a little different than the folks around here."

"Oh, yes, but you're quite entertaining. Skyler thinks you're wonderfully amusing."

Skyler, Skyler, Skyler. The way she said it made Priscilla want to stick out her tongue at the woman. A light of an idea burst in her mind and she spouted it before she thought of the wisdom—or lack thereof—behind it. "Seems like the captain's doing a lot of talking about me."

The air in the room seemed to drop twenty degrees. Priscilla slowed her hands and turned to look at Miss Quartermaine. The woman's countenance was sharp and cold, like an icicle. She opened her mouth to speak—

"All right, are ye ready, m'lady?" Captain Corbett breezed into the room and offered his elbow to Miss Quartermaine. Priscilla spun back around and went right back to her dishes.

As the pair was leaving the kitchen, the captain stopped them in the doorway. Priscilla watched him out of the corner of her eye. He nodded slightly at her. "Dinner was more than passable, Miss Jones. Thank ye for the effort."

"You're welcome."

As they swept out the door, Miss Quartermaine laughed in her light, annoying way and said, "Why, Skyler, if you're in need of a chef, I can send you Pierre. He'd be here in two days, no more than three..."

"Nay, that won't be necessary. Miss Jones has it all in hand."

Priscilla hung on the words as the couple drifted off into the night. He'd paid her a compliment. Finally, and only indirectly, but still, a compliment.

Priscilla's hands moved a little faster and her mood lightened, despite the frigid encounter with Miss Quartermaine. She didn't realize she was humming a hymn as she finished up. So lost in her lighter mood, she gasped when the captain returned to the kitchen.

"Miss Jones, I need to tell ye something, but I wanted ye to be alone."

"Yes." Her mouth went dry as she turned to him and her heart thundered in her chest. Her reaction dismayed and frightened her. "What is it?"

"My father will be paying us a visit tomorrow. I expect we'd both like to have a word with him."

For some reason, Priscilla didn't think this was necessarily good news. It made her spirits droop a little again. Was the captain's father coming to take her home? Only she had no home in her beloved mountains anymore. "I look forward to meeting him," she lied, but what else could she say?

The captain wet his lips and fidgeted for a moment, as if he wanted to add something. Finally, he said, "If ye'll excuse me, Miss Quartermaine is waiting. I'm walking her to the general's."

CHAPTER 15

"You're rather quiet," Danielle said, wrapping her arms tighter around Skyler's elbow. "Are you preoccupied with something?"

"Am I?" Was he? He hadn't been pleased with the note about his father's arrival delivered during dinner. He'd kept the news to himself. Other than sharing it with Miss Jones. She had a right to know, Skyler felt.

"There you go again. You've been drifting off all evening. Aren't you glad to see me?"

Again, a question of which he wasn't sure of the answer. He decided to retreat rather than engage. "There's a lot going on at the fort."

They strolled in silence to the edge of the general's yard, a bright, full moon washing the house and picket fence in shades of silver. "So, where did you find your new house-keeper? She's quite rustic but...charming."

"Aye." He agreed with both descriptors.

Danielle looked up at him expectantly. "You didn't answer the question."

He refrained from a weary sigh. The woman seemed

inordinately curious about Miss Jones. "My father found her. He insisted on making sure there was a woman in the house for the chores, and to assist with Bea." Not a lie, but not the whole truth.

Danielle's expression hardened ever so slightly. Even in the moonlight, the subtle action was obvious. "Your father. How is he?"

"The old goat is a meddling pain in my backside."

"Yes, he made his opinion of me quite clear."

"I'm sorry for that. He speaks his mind." He'd called Danielle a fortune hunter, a woman more interested in family jewels than family ties. That she wanted Skyler more for his title than his soul. Skyler did not believe any of this. Danielle was the daughter of a US senator. In his book, a title as good as lord. He patted her hand. "Perhaps you can win him over yet."

"Hmm." She sounded doubtful, then she cast a glance back over her shoulder toward Skyler's house. "And he found the lovely Miss Jones to keep your house. So good to know he worries about Bea's welfare."

"Aye, that he does. He dotes on his granddaughter."

"Yes. He certainly does."

"Miss Jones is barely above riff-raff, I suppose, but for running the house and keeping Bea out of trouble, she excels."

"She sounds perfect."

The ice in Danielle's tone, however, suggested she meant quite the opposite.

SKYLER DID NOT DALLY at the general's house. He wished Danielle a good night, tossed a salute to the general who was peering through the window, and ambled back toward his home. He sensed Danielle's disappointment. True, he'd been a bit standoffish tonight. He'd not even kissed the woman's cheek to bid her a good evening.

The thought had crossed his mind but with the general's proximity, Skyler hadn't felt it appropriate. And he had been relieved, in an odd way. His mind was not set on Danielle for anything, neither to court nor marry. He hadn't been as glad to see her as he'd thought he would be, either. She fit on his arm. She was beautiful, cultured, intelligent, but often, she was like standing next to an ice sculpture.

This had not bothered him before. Now, suddenly, Danielle seemed a touch...shallow. He dragged a tense hand through his hair. His life, his thoughts, his home were so discombobulated at the moment.

He blamed Miss Jones. The woman was a disruptive force. She was a walking contradiction who challenged Skyler's patience and reason.

An escort would bring his father in tomorrow. Skyler would see to it she left with him. He couldn't have *Calamity Jane* living in his house, regardless of the status of the stage-coach lines—

"Da," Bea called from somewhere off in the shadows.

Skyler tracked his daughter's voice and caught sight of her and Nate strolling across the parade ground. He waved them over. "How was Sergeant Bonhoeffer's fiddle this evening?"

"Oh, he was wonderful," Bea sang, twirling about dreamily.

Skyler cut his eyes at Nate, who raised his hands in defense. "I was by her side the entire time."

"Was the young man—?"

"Yes, but he kept to his own party."

Skyler grunted. "I see." Apparently, just being in the room with the young Private Willoughby was enough to give his daughter clouds for shoes. It was disconcerting to see her so...so smitten. "Ye said ye'd help Miss Jones with the dishes. Ye left her with them all."

Bea's face fell. "Oh, I did. I forgot all about her. I'll go apologize and do extra chores for her tomorrow."

"See that ye do."

The girl flitted into the house and Skyler leaned on the fence to stare up at the stars. "So Willoughby was there?"

"Yes, but I don't think you have to worry about him, Skyler...not yet, anyway."

"Miss Jones said almost the same thing."

"Speaking of Miss Jones, that was pretty callous the way you relegated her to the kitchen. Especially in front of Miss Quartermaine."

"It was not intentional. I spoke with her earlier today and clarified our situation. I assumed she understood."

"Clarified?"

"I'm not looking for a wife, especially one—"

"As rough as Miss Jones. I know."

Skyler raised an eyebrow at the interruption. "I was going to say one my father picked for me."

"Oh." Nate crossed his arms and hunched his shoulders as if Skyler's correction had embarrassed him. "Does that mean you're getting used to her...her backwoods way?"

"I dinnae think any man could get used to that." They both chuckled affably, but then Skyler shook his head. "She's a lovely woman. I see she has a big heart...and unexpected gifts. It's a shame, her background."

"Well, uh..." Nate drifted his knuckles over his chin.

"You're hemming and hawing, mon. Is there something ye want to say?"

"Well, uh—"

"Ye said that."

"I don't know how to broach this subject, Skyler. I think

it's a little more helpful that you've changed your arrangement with Miss Jones, but it's still awkward."

"Mayhap ye could just spit it out and we'll see where it lands."

"All right." Nate nodded, freed his hands, and stood up straighter. "A few of the men have come to me and—well, let me be honest. *Several* men have come to me asking after Miss Jones."

"Aye, I had a jittery, uninvited Private Clark on my porch this morning."

"Yes. They don't know exactly how to approach this, and I had no idea what to say."

"Hmm." Skyler crossed his arms and began to pace. He found the situation annoyed him. He had not been saddled with the woman to now play a shepherd of her virtue. Not that the sassy wench would let him. Not without a fight.

"To the devil with her," he said, pushing off the fence. "I'm sending her back with my father and the escort."

"Back to where?"

"Home to her people in the Highlands."

"Her father sold their place. Gave the money to Miss Jones as a dowry."

Skyler nodded approvingly. A good father was the man, he thought. The money was a pittance, most likely, but he had not sent his daughter off with her hand out. He respected that. It changed his expectation, however, of simply sending her away. "Perhaps she can go back with Da to his ranch then."

Nate shrugged. "An idea. She would probably like the wildness of it. The horses, the mountains, the freedom of it. She loves to ride and shoot."

His insight seemed intimate to Skyler, raising a question. "How is it that ye know so much about her? About the dowry and her skills with a gun?"

"Um...Bea. Bea told me some things."

Skyler held his peace, but he knew when his friend was hedging. And none of it mattered. Tomorrow, Skyler was going to clean up this mess with his father and send Miss Jones packing.

～

PRISCILLA SAT down at her vanity mirror and brushed out her hair with long, slow strokes. Her mind kept going back to Captain Corbett sliding in close to drop the mugs in the sink—so close she could smell the pie on his breath and the scent that was unique to him. It made her pulse race just thinking about him.

She could also feel the daggers in her back from Miss Quartermaine. Priscilla knew a predator when she saw one. She'd be careful around the woman.

"Priscilla?"

Bea appeared in the mirror. "Come on in." Priscilla swiveled on her chair to greet the girl. "You disappeared tonight."

"I'm sorry. I didn't mean to leave you with the work."

"Nah, that ain't what I meant. I just thought you were outside with your pa...and the others."

"I don't like Miss Quartermaine." Bea's shoulders hunched up like she shouldn't admit such a thing, and she sat down on the bed. "She makes me uncomfortable."

"You and me both."

"Nate and I went to listen to Sergeant Bonhoeffer's fiddle."

"Oh, that sounds nice." Priscilla missed fiddle music. Her pa had played.

"Anyway, I think she wants to marry Da," Bea said

abruptly. "If she does, I think she'll send me off to finishing school somewhere."

"I don't know what finishing school is, but I get the feeling she'd like to send me there, too." Priscilla turned back around to the mirror and talked to Bea's reflection. "So...you think your pa wants to marry that icicle?"

Bea chewed on her lip a minute, then shook her head. "I don't know. I used to think so, as she's the only female he lets come around, but..."

"But what?"

"I don't know. He didn't seem himself this evening. Not as relaxed around her. Not as glad to see her."

"He sounded pretty glad, from what I could hear."

"Uh-uh. I know my da. He might be distracted by things at the fort. I'm not sure, but he acted differently toward her tonight."

Priscilla wouldn't dare hope she had anything to do with his unusual behavior and went back to brushing her hair.

"Da, I believe, is going to allow me to attend the gala. But you'll have to go as my babysitter."

"I beg your pardon?"

"My escort. There to keep an eye on me, to make sure I don't go out in the moonlight with Private Willoughby." Her expression took a hard turn. "Not that he would take me. He can't see me in the moonlight. Not as a woman, anyway."

Priscilla huffed a heavy sigh. Men had never caused her so much trouble. "Well, you put on a pretty dress, fix your hair real special, pinch your cheeks, and maybe he'll give it some thought. And then I'll go with you." It was meant as a joke, but Bea had drifted off somewhere.

"Maybe." Suddenly, the girl's eyes went round like a spooked owl. "Priscilla, we've got to get you a gown somewhere."

"A gown? What do I need a gown for?"

"The gala is formal. The men will be in uniform and we have to wear our very best."

"I've got that pretty plaid dress I bought."

Bea's gaze bounced around the ceiling like she was searching for the answer in the rafters. "No. Yes. I mean, if you have to, but...I'd just like to see you give Miss Quartermaine a run for her money."

Priscilla wouldn't mind that either but didn't see a way around the fact she had no fancy gown.

"I'll think of something," Bea muttered, chewing on her thumbnail. "I'll think of something."

BEA WASN'T BLIND, but she kept her notions to herself. She had a feeling meddling in the affairs of adults could be a dangerous thing. She slipped beneath her covers and wiggled happily down into her feather mattress. But she *wanted* to meddle. Fiddle music still played in her head and she sighed over Private Willoughby. He did not look at her the way she'd caught her da looking at Priscilla.

When he thought no one was looking, he watched her. And he seemed almost a little jittery when they talked—a thing he tried to cover up with yelling.

Priscilla watched him the same way. Wide-eyed, dewy, snatching her gaze away when Da looked at her.

Miss Quartermaine had watched them both with eyes glittering with jealousy. Nothing got by that woman. If she suspected Da was developing a warm feeling for Priscilla, then she would try to stop it. Bea understood this instinctively, but did Priscilla? Did she understand she needed to be careful around the woman?

Bea determined that she would discuss her fears with Nate. He was a good listener and offered wise counsel. She had another idea as well, and fell asleep with a smile on her face.

~

THE NEXT MORNING, she scurried over to Nate's, knocking lightly on his door. Miss Yahtzen, a skinny German woman with a stern face, opened up. A stern face but a smile softened it greatly. "Good morning, Bea," she said through her thick accent. "Do you come to see Lieutenant Owens?"

"Yes, please."

"Come on in, Bea," he called from the kitchen. "Have some flap jacks."

"Oh, I think I will." She gave Miss Yahtzen a hopeful look.

"Come, I make you fresh, hot ones."

~

SITUATED with a plate of flapjacks and a cup of coffee in front of her, Bea wanted to dive in but refrained for the moment. After all, she'd come on business. "I like Miss Jones, don't you?" She poured some syrup on her breakfast, making sure it soaked the bacon.

"Yes, I do. She's a lovely young woman with a good heart and strong character."

Bea took a bite to buy herself a minute to get her words right. "I think she likes Da. And I think Da likes her."

Nate paused with a strip of bacon halfway to his mouth. He narrowed his eyes at her. "What makes you say that?"

"I catch them sneaking looks at one another. But for Da, it was Miss Quartermaine that made me really consider the notion. He didn't treat her the same last night as he has."

Bea would have almost sworn a smile tried to break on

Nate's face, but he took a bite of bacon quickly and spoke while he crunched on it. "I might have noticed something, myself."

"Well, the gala is coming up and Priscilla doesn't have a nice enough dress for it, but I have an idea on how to get her one."

"It disappoints me, Bea, how much you and your father worry about how Miss Jones makes you look."

"How she makes *me* look? No. I know she was a little embarrassing at first in her britches, but I am worried about *her* now. I don't want her going to the gala without a nice dress and have Miss Quartermaine make her feel..."

"You want to get her a party dress so she...?"

"Can feel pretty. She is, you know. Just as pretty as Miss Quartermaine, maybe prettier."

"I wouldn't disagree."

"So, I have an idea, and I came to tell you about it."

Nate straightened attentively in his chair. "I am all ears."

CHAPTER 16

THE EARLY AFTERNOON SUN BEAT DOWN ON TOP OF BEA'S head as she waited. Da, Nate, the general, Miss Quartermaine's party, and Priscilla all stood with her on the porch in front of the fort office. She could hear the thunder of the approaching horses, and a dust cloud rose up above the fort wall. Growing warm, she stepped back to find shade. How foolish of her to have forgotten her hat.

A guard yelled from the walk, "Open up the gate. Escort approaching."

Two men jumped to the task. Sergeant Bonhoeffer moved away a few feet to give them room to work. The gates swung open and butterflies burst free in Bea's stomach.

She tugged on her shirtwaist and brushed off her skirt. She wanted to look lovely for Grand Da, lovely and mature. She raised her chin and glanced over at Private Willoughby, standing guard at the bottom of the steps.

The escort of fifty men and horses surrounding the stage slowed their trot to a walk and entered the fort, but still, the dust was a choking mess. Miss Quartermaine grimaced and turned her head, as if that would protect her. Priscilla blinked but kept her eyes on the stage in the midst of the blue uniforms. Da, Nate, Henry, Jack, and Private Willoughby barely reacted at all. Bea smiled at their ruggedness.

Lieutenant Klovenak rode up to the group on a pretty sorrel and saluted the officers. Da and Nate saluted back. "Any problems, lieutenant?" her father asked.

"No, sir. We saw some sign out near Bowler Pass and dispatched the scouts. They have as yet not rejoined us."

Her father nodded, but a deep groove etched itself into his forehead. "Thank you. You may dismiss your men."

"Thank you, sir." He saluted again and yelled the order to disband. The soldiers rode off, stirring up a little more dust.

Private Willoughby approached the stage and opened the door. "Lord Corbett, nice to see you again."

Grand Da slowly made his way out of the stage. He was a big man, tall, thick, with broad shoulders. He was athletic, though, and agile. He squeezed his mass through the carriage door and jumped to the ground like a spry giant leaping down from the beanstalk. "Private, good to see you." Grand Da commenced to knocking the dust off his clothes. Not an insignificant amount. A small cloud swirling after each pat, he looked up and grinned at his son. "Corbett, my boy, it's been too long."

The two met on the middle step and shook hands, Grand Da's motion more joyful than Da's. "Aye, Father, it's good to have ye here. How are things up in Montana?"

Bea could tell by her father's cool tone and stiff expression he was, in truth, less than pleased to see Grand Da. Grand Da, however, did not seem to care or notice.

"Fine, fine," he said, loud and full of might. "Herd is growing at a breakneck pace."

Returning to the porch, bringing Grand Da with him, Skyler motioned to the group. "I think you know everyone."

The men exchanged greetings, friendly and lighthearted. Their laughter was deep and manly, and Bea grinned at them. Grand Da went down the line, paused ever so slightly at Miss Quartermaine before he took her hand and kissed it. "Lovely as ever, my dear."

"Thank you, Lord Corbett. Lovely to see you, also."

Then it was Bea's turn. She stood straighter, raised her chin, and smiled broadly at her grandfather. "Grand Da, I have missed you."

"Is that how you greet yer grandfather that ye haven't seen in months?"

Bea needed no prompting. She jumped into her grandfather's arms and he swung her around with joyous laughter. "I've missed my girl." When he set her down, he frowned, cocked his head, and took a step back. "Girl? My, ye've grown into a beautiful, beautiful lady just over spring. Are ye married yet?"

Everyone laughed, especially Bea, and she flicked a glance at Private Willoughby, who was smiling with the rest of the group. "Not yet, Grand Da."

He pinched her cheek. "Don't be in too much of a hurry, lass. Before ye know it, ye'll be old and gray like meself."

"And this young lady," Skyler motioned to Priscilla. "Miss—"

"Priscilla Jones." Grand Da nearly pushed Da out of the way as he positioned himself directly in front of her and took both her hands. "I've heard so much about ye, I feel as if I know ye."

"Reckon you have the advantage over me, sir."

Grand Da kissed both her hands. "Not for long, I wager. I have been so eager to meet the wild cat of Ocoee County. Oh, the stories Dr. Owens has shared with me." He looked heavenward and laughed. "Tall tales, if ever I heard one. Only..." Grand Da looked at Bea and winked. "Only, I think they're true, Bea, my wee bairn. What say ye?"

"I say they're true, too."

"We shall all have a grand time at the gala tomorrow night hearing some of them. Miss Jones, I must be yer first dance—"

"Oh, Grand Da—" Bea interrupted. "I'm so sorry. Miss Jones and I can't attend."

"What the devil?" He dropped one of Priscilla's hands and turned to Bea. "Why can't ye come? Ye're old enough now."

"Well, Da has said I can't go unless I have an appropriate escort—which should be Miss Jones. However, Miss Jones came to us with a limited wardrobe and she doesn't have a dress appropriate for the event."

The group fell silent. Priscilla blushed and sputtered sounds but no words. Grand Da sputtered as well, took a step back, but did not relinquish her hand. "There must be something..." He passed his gaze over the group and back again, then once more... "Something we can do..." And he landed on Miss Quartermaine. Everyone else followed his lead.

Miss Quartermaine, for a moment, lost her regal bearing as her mouth moved but didn't issue coherent sounds.

Priscilla blushed a startling shade of crimson. "Oh, now. Bea and I will figure something out."

But the rest of the group stayed on Miss Quartermaine, who struggled to regain her composure, as her gaze bounced about the faces. Finally, she raised her chin. "You've nothing to worry about, Miss Jones. I can certainly provide you with an appropriate gown—"

"Oh, I couldn't—"

"I insist. I absolutely insist. Bea well knows I travel with three trunks." She passed a quick glance over Bea and surveyed Priscilla from bottom to top. "I'm sure I have something that will fit, even if there is a little room...up top."

Nate's brow rose and he, like the other men, suddenly found the porch, the ceiling, the busy fort enthralling. Anywhere these women weren't. Bea and Grand Da, however, did not look away. Bea was almost surprised by the meanness of the comment. Almost.

Grand Da only chuckled and returned his attention to Priscilla. "I'm sure ye'll be the belle of the ball, even if ye wear buckskins."

Priscilla blinked, shook her head, then nodded at Miss Quartermaine. "Thank you, ma'am."

"My pleasure."

"Aye, lass," Grand Da said, tugging on Priscilla's hand, "are ye up for a walk?"

"Oh, I'd love one." For a moment, Bea thought Priscilla might kiss Grand Da right there on the porch, the look of relief was so obvious on her face.

Da frowned as the couple left the porch, Grand Da talking fast as a wound-up clock, Priscilla clinging to his arm. Bea puffed up like a rooster. Not only had her plan to get Priscilla a dress worked, but the woman had remembered a certain lesson in etiquette. When a man offers his arm to escort you, always take it, Bea had told her. And there she was, strolling with Grand Da like a lady.

"Well, it seems as if I have an assignment," Miss Quartermaine said, picking up her hem. "I'll go find Miss Jones a dress." She whirled away but then seemed to slow her walk on purpose.

Da wrinkled his face up but quickly righted it. "Here,

yes, I should escort ye back to the house." He squeezed Nate's shoulder as he stepped past him but spoke to the general. "I'll be along momentarily, sir. Nate will see that ye're comfortable."

"Very good."

"All right," Nate said.

Henry and Jack tagged each other on the shoulder and grinned. "Hot day," Jack said.

"Good day for a beer," Henry said. Laughing like hyenas, the two leaped from the porch and scurried toward town.

As the group disbanded, Nate leaned down to Bea's ear. "Looks like your plan worked. Miss Jones has a dress."

"And every man in this fort is going to want to dance with her when they see her in one of Miss Quartermaine's fancy gowns."

He straightened up and glanced back to Da and Miss Quartermaine. "Yes, they will, won't they, Bea?"

"Yes."

"Now it's your turn to help me with a plan. I'll find you in a little while."

Priscilla matched her pace to Lord Corbett's, rested her hand lightly on his arm as Bea had taught her, and listened politely to his tale of traveling from his ranch to the fort. She was, however, dying to interrupt him and ask how he knew her pa.

They passed under the shade of a large cottonwood, and he paused his story to pull a silk handkerchief from his pocket. "It's warm down here." He patted his glistening forehead. "I prefer the mountains, myself."

"I miss mine something fierce."

The old man turned to her. He reminded Priscilla of a

well-dressed, friendly bear, as he was a big man but struck her as gentle. "Lass, what do ye think of things here in the fort? Of my son?"

She took a deep breath to steal a moment to think. She had trouble putting words to everything she felt. But, then, what she felt didn't matter. "Lord Corbett, I ain't—I'm *not* the right kind of woman for your son. He wants somebody like Miss Quartermaine."

Corbett waved a hand back and forth in frustration. "My son doesn't know what he wants. He's put his life on a shelf as if he should suffer somehow for his wife's death."

"Maybe. All I know is he doesn't want me around. And, honestly, I don't cotton to being somebody's housekeeper all my life."

"But ye promised yer father."

"I did. And if Captain Corbett had been willing to honor the arrangement, I would have done my best to stick. Strikes me, though, that there's no bargain if only one party is willing to shake on it."

"He's not willing to shake on it?"

"No."

Lord Corbett hung his head. "Foolish, foolish man."

"Oh, I don't blame him. When I set myself next to Miss Quartermaine, well, I can see how I don't fit."

"Nonsense, girl. Ye've more character and compassion in yer little finger than that icicle has in her whole body."

"You speak your mind, don't you?"

Corbett leaned in a little and winked. "Aye, I do, and I will."

"Then tell me how and why I'm here. You seemed to know I wasn't exactly gonna fit your son like a glove."

He looked away, pale-blue eyes frosting over. Priscilla watched, fascinated by the emotions that drifted across his face. His brow creased with sadness, then the side of his mouth lifted into a curl. "I knew a girl—a bonnie lass—from the highlands of Scotland. She was rough, uneducated, but smart as a whip, tough as rawhide. She stole my heart."

"What happened?"

He came back to her and winked. "I married her. She was Skyler's mother."

"Ooh." Priscilla thought she understood. "You thought he'd see me the same way?"

He shook his head, the troubled crease returning. "His mother endured years of scandal until the gossips finally got tired. She was accepted into society and her past was forgotten. Skyler never knew this about her. He only knew her as a Lady and, therefore, has no appreciation for what makes a real woman."

"So you raised a snob...and my pa raised a girl who ain't —*isn't*—fit for proper society."

Corbett chuckled, offered his arm, and they started walking again. "Aye, I suppose that was the truth of it. But looking at ye now, I can see one of the mistakes has been rectified."

"Bea's helping me with my talk and other ladylike ways."

"By the looks of it, she's doing a fine job."

"I don't know. I reckon."

"What's the matter?"

Priscilla didn't know where to begin. "How'd you hear all the stuff about me that you seem to know?"

"Lieutenant Owens's father is a good friend. Dr. Owens wrote me when your father was, uh, getting short on his days. He told me about ye. I considered the situation and Skyler's temperament and gave it my blessing."

"You should have told Captain Corbett."

"And spoil all the fun? Tell me, did ye really steal your horse back from a group of Cherokee braves?"

"He was my horse."

Lord Corbett threw his head back and laughed. This man's feather-headed attitude about Priscilla's life sparked a flame in her. "And what fun? Since I've got here, I've had to put two drunks in their place. Poked my fingers full of holes learning needlepoint. Passed off the stares of men who ain't never seen a woman in britches. Captain Corbett yells all the time. About everything. I can't go barefoot. I can't go riding or shooting or hunting. There's no fun here at all except for—" She stopped. Teaching Bea to throw a knife was a secret.

"Except for?"

"Bea. I enjoy her company right much."

Lord Corbett sagged a little and shook his head. "I'm sorry. I was being selfish. I thought ye'd make yer way work here."

"I miss Pa. I miss my mountains. I miss feeling the grass beneath—" She licked her lips and stopped right there. A tightening in her throat warned her of the whining. She sniffed, wiggled her nose, and started again. "The captain don't want me, and I reckon that frees me from my promise to Pa. When the stage opens up, I'll take my dowry...and... and go someplace else."

I'm being a crybaby, Lord, but this is too hard. I sure as heck won't keep house for him and Miss Quartermaine. I'd rather eat dirt.

"Miss Jones," Lord Corbett began gently, "my son is a hard-headed man at times, but he is not lacking in intelligence. I beg ye to give him time to see yer worth...and the cost of his foolish pride."

"Time? Until the stagecoach line opens up, I reckon time is what I've got."

～

"WHAT DO you think of Grand Da?" Bea asked, flouncing down on Priscilla's bed that evening.

Priscilla looked up from the little desk where she was practicing her writing and shook her head. "I've met tornadoes with less force."

"I know. He's something…so, I've come to work on your dancing."

Seemed like all the spirit and life had flowed out of Priscilla. She was wilting, like a flower in need of water. "It's late, and I'm—"

"Just ten minutes?" The girl batted her long lashes at Priscilla and laced her hands together as if in prayer. She was adorable and Priscilla wondered how Miss Quartermaine could so easily overlook her.

"All right." She didn't see the point. Whether she could or couldn't dance didn't affect Skyler's opinion one way or the other.

"Well, don't sound so excited."

"Bea…" Priscilla put down her pencil and pivoted in her chair to face the girl. "Things ain't—aren't—working out here. I'm just in the way. And I know I promised my pa, but your pa isn't interested in the deal. Soon as the stagecoach is running again, I'm going to head on to somewhere else."

Bea dropped her head and traced a flower in the quilt for several seconds before she responded. "I want you to stay, Priscilla, but I understand, I think. You can't stay if Da courts or marries Miss Quartermaine. Is that it?"

Priscilla had no desire to voice any of the unexpected feelings Skyler Corbett brought to the surface of her heart. She didn't understand them herself, but Bea's understanding gaze and sweet smile worked one word free. "Yes."

Bea grunted and went back to tracing the flower. "He just needs to see…to see you're every bit a lady as she is."

Priscilla snorted. "That's not true."

"It could be."

Priscilla thought of her conversation with Lord Corbett and the story of his wife. But did she want to turn into a lady and leave behind the way she'd been raised, the things she loved about being Priscilla Jones?

She just wasn't sure anymore.

CHAPTER 17

SKYLER PACED UP AND DOWN THE FRONT PORCH, BARELY ABLE to contain his anger with his father, especially since he'd been holding it in all day. "I cannae believe ye'd play with people's lives like this. Ye've overstepped, and she'll be going back with ye."

Lord Corbett froze with the match's flame right at the bowl of his pipe. "How's that, ye say?"

Skyler spun on his father. "She has no one and no home. I don't want her here. Ye've right properly set her up in an impossible situation."

"Nate tells me the woman cut a bullet out of ye." Lord Corbett casually lit his pipe, then tossed the dead match off the porch into the darkness.

"So? I got scratched." He reflexively touched his side. "She doctored me."

"Scratched?"

"The bullet barely was in my skin. Don't make so much of it. I'm almost healed."

"Do ye think yer Ice Princess Miss Quartermaine would have had the fortitude to do such a thing?"

"Nay, and I wouldn't have asked her to."

"So, ye would have died from a bullet to keep yer blood from staining her pretty, little hands?"

"Da, it's my life. Ye've overstepped thinking ye can pick a wife for me. I'll not have it."

"Oh, so that's the problem."

"What?"

"If I hadn't stepped in and sent ye the Highland bride, ye might would have seen her in a different light."

"Ye call her a Highland bride as if she were some bloody princess. She's a ragamuffin. A-a farmer's daughter."

Corbett sucked on the pipe, exhaled slowly, thoughtfully. "I've raised a right good effete snob. If I didn't know better, I'd swear ye're English."

"That's a low blow. Would ye really want that girl—" Skyler caught himself and lowered his voice. "Would ye really want her as a daughter-in-law? Would she not embarrass ye around ye're lordly friends?"

A mysterious twinkle glimmered in his father's eyes, made more haunting by the bright moonlight. "Me, no. You, apparently, yes. Besides, we've not had any lordly visitors at the ranch since yer mother passed. Ten years now."

Exasperated, Skyler leaned back on the rail. "I don't understand what possessed ye to do this thing. But I'll be expecting ye to undo it."

"The girl needed help. Ye needed a wife."

"Not that badly."

Lord Corbett exhaled smoke rings and the men watched them drift away in the cool night air. "Ye're raising Bea now without so much as a nod to God. How do ye think that will turn out?"

"God," Skyler whispered. "I don't know Him anymore, and I don't feel the loss."

"Because ye're angry."

"Yes, I'm angry. Louisa shouldn't have died."

"Louisa was delicate," Corbett said gently, evenly. "I feared this would be a challenging post for her."

"But I took it, and now she's gone."

"Is that it? Guilt? Ye blame yerself?"

Skyler didn't answer. He and God were responsible for her death. But punishing himself was all the control over the matter that he had.

"Lad," Corbett laid a hand on Skyler's shoulder. "Life and death go hand-in-hand with our choices. All we can do is pray to make the best ones available to us. Louisa never blamed ye for her life. She dinnae blame ye for her death, either."

Skyler was tired. He was tired of this guilt. He was tired of wondering if he'd given his career more of himself than his family. He was concerned the patrols had not been able to pick up One-Who-Cries's trail. Settlers were dying. The army was losing ground. Added to all these swirling cares, he was here arguing with his father about a woman that, if he'd let her, could scramble his good sense.

"Miss Jones leaves with ye after the gala. And I think I'll send Bea to stay with ye for a bit..." *Before I send her off to school.*

"Why? Not that I wouldn't want her, but why now?"

"We've got trouble to put an end to. I need to take command of the patrols. I don't want to be worrying about my girl worrying about me."

"Ye think she'll worry less if she's in a different state?"

"Ye'll keep her busy. I know ye. She adores yer company. By fall, if I'm fortunate, I'll have One-Who-Cries in chains or buried." And Bea will be older and more of a temptation for the men. Finishing school was the remedy. "Enjoy the summer with her."

Corbett huffed a long, weary sigh. "So be it."

～

PRISCILLA HAD NEVER EVEN DREAMED such a beautiful dress could exist. She tried to hide her awe as Miss Quartermaine draped the gown over the bed. It was the blue of a Carolina sky, and a fabric as sheer as a mist covered the skirt. Dainty pearls lined the shoulders and neckline. The dress was the most beautiful, feminine thing Priscilla had ever been close to, and she reached out to drift her fingers over the bodice.

"Stunning, isn't it?" Miss Quartermaine said softly.

But Priscilla heard the hiss of Satan in her voice and pulled her hand back. "Why are you doing this?"

Green eyes, cold and bottomless, sparkled with mirth. Her lips twitched ever so slightly. "For one, I had no choice. Bea maneuvered me into this."

Priscilla blinked in surprise at the woman's honesty.

Miss Quartermaine chuckled and sashayed to the door. "Then I realized, this is the least I can do to—for—you. I'll see you this evening, Miss Jones."

～

BEA REACHED out and twirled one strand of Priscilla's hair around her finger to tighten a curl. "There. You're beautiful."

Priscilla tilted her head and smiled at Bea. The girl was beautiful, as well, and looked so grown up with all her red curls piled high upon her head. The dress of pink silk fit her snugly and featured a fetching bustle. "So are you. You look very mature."

The girl's own smile spread exponentially, but Priscilla tapped her on the nose. "Don't get carried away. My job is to watch you like a hawk."

"I know, I know, but Nate said he'd watch me while you

dance. Honestly, this is embarrassing. I don't need *watching*. I'm almost fifteen."

"And as pretty as a picture. I've seen what pretty does to men."

"Ladies," Captain Corbett bellowed in his usual, friendly voice. "We must go. I expect ye're ready."

Priscilla picked up a filmy, gauzy shawl, amazed at its almost angelic appearance. "I expect we better be."

SKYLER HAD GOTTEN USED to seeing Miss Jones in dresses, therefore he had no concern she would distract him...but the woman he saw drifting down the stairs in a blue ball gown took away his breath. She'd curled her golden hair and lovely little strands of it hung about her shoulders. Some of it had been pinned up and baby's breath peeked out here and there. The color of the gown made her eyes sparkle, her skin glow, her cheeks reflect a rosy pink.

She did indeed remind him of—

"A Highland bride," his father whispered, nudging him in the ribs. "Ye're a fool, Skyler. A terrible, burning fool."

Skyler glared at his father. "I'll be on the porch."

PRISCILLA TRIED to hide the hurt that pierced her heart as Skyler stormed out. For a moment, she'd thought she'd seen something warm, even affectionate, in his gaze. And she'd noticed how handsome and trim he looked in his dress blues. She'd offered a shaky smile, at which point he'd hardened like day-old bread and turned away.

Trying to recover from the snub, she smiled at Lord Corbett when he offered up his gloved hand. He, too, was dressed to impress in a fine, tailored tuxedo and glistening leather shoes.

"My dear, ye're most enchanting. Angelic, I'd dare say." He looked past her and grinned at Bea. "And who is this beautiful, mysterious woman with ye?"

Bea nearly floated off the stairs. "Grand Da, do you like it?" She stepped into the middle of the foyer and twirled, a gown of pale pink silk glimmering in the overhead lantern. She was beautiful, and Priscilla felt like a proud mother.

The thought hurt her heart. She'd grown so attached to the girl.

"I'm the most fortunate man at the gala," Lord Corbett said, offering up his elbows. "I get the first dance with each of ye."

CHAPTER 18

PRISCILLA HAD NOT MADE IT TO ANY OF THE DANCES BACK IN Ocoee, so the gala was quite the shock. The Baptist church was the largest building in the area. All the pews were gone, candles and lanterns burned brightly overhead, shimmering like starlight, and festive, red-white-and-blue shawls hung all along the walls.

Banjos and fiddles and harmonicas twanged and dueled, erupting together in infectious, toe-tapping music. Men dressed smartly in their cleaned uniforms and women in beautiful, glistening gowns were skipping and spinning to a square dance tune when Priscilla and her group arrived. Laughter and music reached the rafters in a deafening but inviting surge.

"Oh, my," she whispered, awed by the lively scene.

"I know," Bea said loudly to be heard over the music. "Isn't it exciting?"

"Yes."

"Here." Bea handed Priscilla a little card with a pencil attached by a ribbon. "This is your dance card. Nate and I took the liberty of filling it out for you."

Priscilla had never seen one of these. It was a list of names. Men and their ranks. She scanned it quickly, disappointed that Captain Corbett was not on the list. She did, however, recognize a few of the names.

Her first dance, as promised, went to Lord Corbett. "Do ye know this dance, lass?"

"I do indeed." She winked at Bea.

"Excellent." He grabbed her and Bea's hands and led them both out. For the first time in months, Priscilla laughed with unbridled joy and let the squawk of the fiddle sweep her back to her mountains. As she skipped, sashayed, and promenaded, she could almost smell the scent of wild roses and mountain laurel and feel the kiss of cool, sweet summer air. She missed Pa, she missed home, but for the moment, she was almost there. Things would have been perfect if she could have kept her gaze on the dancers instead of scanning the crowd, looking for Captain Corbett.

When the song ended, Lord Corbett wiped his brow and bowed to the ladies. "That was delightful."

"Oh, Grand Da, it was! It was. I could dance all night."

"Not with me, ye won't. Nate will be the mon for that. May I get you ladies some punch?"

"I'm right parched after that," Priscilla said, still breathing a little heavy. "Punch would be nice."

As the lord left, Sergeant Bonhoeffer stepped up. "Might I have the next dance, Miss Jones?"

Priscilla looked at Nate. "What about Bea?"

"I will not leave her. Go and enjoy yourself, if you can. Sergeant Bonhoeffer has two left feet."

From then on, soldier after soldier approached Priscilla. Bea and Nate both leaned in and encouraged her to mark off each gentleman's name. The night slipped into an array of friendly, eager faces. Lord Corbett insisted on watching over Bea so Priscilla and Nate could dance together or at the same time with other partners.

By her sixth dance, Priscilla was exhausted and in need of more punch. Private Easterday offered to fetch it for her and Bea. Nate went off to dance with someone named Rose Calhoun, and Lord Corbett took Miss Quartermaine for a turn.

Quite warm, Priscilla fanned herself with her dance card and continued to look for Captain Corbett. She'd spotted him a time or two chatting with Miss Quartermaine, but most of the evening, he'd been engaged in conversations with the general and other officers. Their dour expressions said they had weighty things on their minds. Was this why his name was not on her card? Or had he declined?

"Bea," she said, leaning in so the girl could hear, "who picked the names for my dance card?"

"I told you. Nate and I did. Is something wrong?"

Priscilla didn't want to sound like a whiny crybaby, but she was curious. Maybe his absence was about Miss Quartermaine. "Well, I was just a little curious about your pa and why he, you know, isn't on there." She felt her cheeks warm, and it wasn't the room.

Bea giggled and leaned in even closer. "It was Nate's idea not to put him on there. He said for me—us—to trust him."

SKYLER DANCED WITH DANIELLE, well aware his attention was elsewhere. He had one woman in his arms and a totally different one on his mind. Miss Jones had been downright stunning in her gown, and he felt sure the image would affect him for days, perhaps even more so than the *other* image. He grew a little flushed thinking about her. Such a conundrum. She never ceased to surprise him with her skills and her charms.

He glanced down and smiled at Danielle as he whirled her about the floor. "A lovely gala, don't ye think?" And a perfect waste of time. He should be planning to find One-Who-Cries, not dillydallying with silly females. But, she was leaving...

"I think it's horrendous, and there's an ostrich sitting in the corner."

"Yes, I agree," he said, his mind roaring down two completely different tracks of thought. *A good way to get killed*, he scolded. He had to gather his wits about him.

After a moment, he realized Danielle was glaring at him. "I'm sorry. Ye were saying?"

Her lips thinned into a sharp line fraught with displeasure. "I was saying I seem to be boring you."

"No, not at all." But a flicker of a sapphire skirt caught his eye and he tracked it up to Miss Jones's face. A few feet away, she was smiling, laughing, having a wonderful time in the arms of Lieutenant Hixson. "I have a renegade Indian that is consuming my thoughts. I apologize for my distraction."

"An Indian?" Danielle did not sound convinced.

Frankly, Skyler was past caring. The song ended and he stepped back. "Thank you, Miss Quartermaine. I'm sure your dance card is full for the rest of the evening."

Before she could argue, if she was going to, Skyler was off on a mission. One way to clear his mind was to take at least one of his distractions head-on. One dance with Miss Jones. A goodbye, as it were. Lieutenant Whitby was about to lead her out for a dance when he approached from behind. Skyler tapped his officer on the shoulder. "May I cut in?"

The man silently mouthed his surprise, and a pinch in

his brow expressed his disappointment, but he glanced at Skyler's lapel and nodded. "Yes, sir. Of course."

Skyler slipped his hand into Miss Jones's and draped his arm around her waist. It amazed him how natural she felt to him. Her cheeks flamed and she looked away. The sassy thing had a bashful side. Did he have an effect on her? He was grateful for a low, soft waltz so they could hear each other without yelling. "Are ye enjoying the dance?"

"I am." She licked her lips, seemed to think about something, and then added, "The ladies and their gowns have presented a beautiful palette of colors here tonight, like flowers in a meadow."

Skyler couldn't keep the surprise from his face. "How eloquent of ye."

She blushed a little deeper and shook her head. "I can't take credit. Bea made me memorize it. It's from one of her ladies' magazines."

He chuckled. "In spite of our differences, Miss Jones, I want to thank ye for the time you have spent with my daughter." He knew he should tell her she would be leaving. And he would. Later.

"Please, call me Priscilla. And Bea is a fine young lady. I've learned a lot from her about being a lady. Among a few other things, she taught me to dance."

Would the surprises never stop with this woman and his daughter? "Ye didn't know how?"

Priscilla shook her head. "Never learned. And I only know this box step, so don't go and expect anything fancy."

"I shall share a secret with ye. This is the only dance I know."

"I guess I feel some better then." She smiled and Skyler was mystified by a strange feeling in his chest. Almost like… butterflies fluttering to life. "How is your side?"

The wound. "Ye're as good a nurse as ye're an artist."

She fluttered her lashes at him, a simple, bashful reaction utterly without guile, and he was warmed by it.

"Thank you," she said.

They danced a few steps in silence as he tried to form the words to a heartfelt apology for his poor manners... pointless now that she would be leaving. "I have made a number of missteps with ye. Misjudged ye on more than one occasion. I'm sorry."

"Well, that sounds a little more sincere than the first time you tried to apologize. That's all right. I don't hold a grudge."

"Ye look...beautiful tonight, and I should have had the manners to say so. I know a woman goes to much trouble for these events. Compliments are the mark of...success." He ended awkwardly there, lamenting his lack of eloquence.

Priscilla seemed to ponder the compliment. "You really think I look beautiful?"

Skyler almost laughed at her question. She sounded honestly befuddled by his compliment. "Has no one ever told ye that before?"

She shrugged as they whirled around the floor. "Maybe a long time ago, at church or somewhere. I'm not sure. I can only recall my pa telling me how pretty I was every now and then."

"I don't think I even offered my condolences on the passing of yer father. I'm sorry for that, and your loss, as well."

"I miss him, but it gets a little better every day."

"Aye, the pain never goes away. It just becomes a part of ye, and ye move forward."

"I'm sorry about your wife. Bea told me she was sick for a spell."

"Tuberculosis. We thought she was recovering at one point, and then she passed suddenly." *Feverish, incoherent, coughing up blood, she died in my arms.* "This is no country for gentle women."

She looked out at the other dancers, a pensive pinch in her brow, and he felt badly for the somber conversation. This was the only dance he would have with the little Highland bride. He did not want it to end badly. "How is it that no man back in Ocoee had the good sense to marry a woman who can knit, draw, wield a knife, and remove bullets?"

Priscilla laughed richly, the sound of it wrapping Skyler's soul in a comforting, peaceful embrace. The feeling surprised him.

"My lands," she said, amusement lacing her voice, "can I do all that?"

Her joy was infectious and he joined her. "In my book, ye'd be quite the catch if ye'd learn to bridle yer tongue and wear shoes."

Her laughter ended suddenly, her expression darkened, and her direct gaze pierced him. "You can't have it both ways, Captain." He wondered if he'd imagined a tremble in her chin. "I'm countrified, remember? An embarrassment. Not a lady."

"Priscilla, I didn't—"

The music ended and the dancers clapped. "We'll be taking a break now, folks," the banjo player informed them.

Skyler held on to her, suddenly loathsome of letting her go. "I...I..."

She tilted her head, waiting. What was he trying to say? She *was* countrified. Yet, this seemed less of a problem than before. But this was no place for women. He couldn't go through that again.

She slipped free of his grasp. "Thank you for the dance."

BEA WAS RETURNING from the lady's room, weaving her way through the crowd, when she overheard Miss Quartermaine laugh and mention Priscilla. Knowing she shouldn't, Bea sidled up close enough to eavesdrop. The band was on a break and so she heard quite clearly.

"Yes, I understand she can throw a knife like an Indian. Alarmingly accurate. You should ask her to demonstrate, Private. I'm sure it would be entertaining."

Bea cut off a gasp. How did Miss Quartermaine know about the knife throwing?

Private Henderson laughed and slapped the soldier next to him. "I'd pay to see it. I've heard all kinds of crazy stories about her. She's a real Calamity Jane."

Bea slipped away amid the laughter, vaguely uncomfortable Miss Quartermaine was discussing Priscilla. Pushing through the forest of uniforms and pretty gowns, she was looking for Nate when Priscilla tapped her on the shoulder. "Can you direct me to the lady's room?"

Bea changed direction and took Priscilla's arm. "I'll show you." She wanted to warn her about Miss Quartermaine.

They were busy pardoning and excusing their way through the crowd when Private Henderson approached Priscilla. "Ma'am, I'm on your dance card. Private Henderson. I was wondering, while the band's on a break, if you had a moment, could you settle a bet for me and my friend here?"

Private Willoughby emerged from the crowd and Bea's heart lunged to a gallop. "I bet Private Henderson here, Miss Jones, that you can throw a knife like some folks throw darts."

Priscilla backed up a touch. "Where'd you hear that, Private Willoughby?"

"Aw, people talk. Is it a rumor, or is there any truth to it?"

"It's true," Bea interjected with too much enthusiasm and lowered her voice. "It's true, and she's teaching me. You should see her throw."

The privates begged Priscilla with their eyes to demonstrate. She glanced at Bea, who nodded eagerly. "You think I should?" she asked.

Bea flicked her eyes at Private Willoughby. "Oh, yes. Please."

She sighed softly. "All right. Just a few throws."

"Excellent," Private Henderson said, motioning toward a door at the back of the room. "Right this way."

She followed him, and Private Willoughby fell in beside Bea. "Are you joshing? Are you learning to throw a knife, too?"

Bea's chest puffed up. "I am, and I'm pretty good."

"Really? Imagine..."

SOMETHING about this felt vaguely wrong to Priscilla, but she did enjoy throwing her knives. She suspected a lady wouldn't give in to this temptation. Miss Quartermaine certainly wouldn't. But then again, she probably wouldn't have been capable of digging a bullet out of Captain Corbett. Still stinging from the painful conversation with him, she decided she could and would do what she wanted, whether he liked it or not.

She followed Private Henderson out of the back door to a clearing where a wagon sat, unhitched and forlorn in the dark. "Dang," he whispered, turning to Private Willoughby. "It's too dark out here. Ma'am, I know you can't—"

"Hang on," Willoughby interrupted. "Give me a second."

He rushed back inside to the party and returned a moment later with two lanterns and two more couples, apparently eager to watch the demonstration, too. While the two privates cast about for places to hang the lanterns—one found a hook at the back door of the church—the other surveyed the area.

"Priscilla, what are you going to throw?" Bea asked. "You didn't bring your knife. Did you?"

"No, I reckoned these boys here would have something."

"Here, ma'am." One of the soldiers to just join them freed a knife from his hip. "Will this do?"

A bone-handled knife with a blade about six inches long. Similar to her own. Priscilla felt the weight of it in her hand, tossed it up into the air a few times. "I'll need to get used to it, but I think it'll work."

"How's this?" Willoughby asked. He raised the tongue on the wagon to an upright position and hung the lantern there.

Priscilla looked around the church's backyard. The only thing in it, besides the wagon, was a tall oak about two feet in diameter. She strode about for several seconds, shifting positions, trying to get both lanterns behind her and remove the glare from her eyes. Finally, she settled on a spot. She could hit the tree, only a dozen or so feet away, but she needed a target. "Private Henderson, can you hang your hat on the oak?"

"My hat? Why mine?"

"Didn't you bet against me? That means you don't think I can hit it."

He huffed a little disgusted sound but marched over to the tree and pulled his kepi from his belt. It took the hat a little convincing, but it finally stayed put, the wool caught just enough in the oak's bark to keep it still.

Priscilla stepped a touch closer, about ten or so feet from the target, and rolled her shoulders. The dress pulled some, but she figured she'd have enough movement. "Three chances to hit it."

"Three?" Henderson whined.

"This ain't—*isn't*—my knife, and I've never thrown in a dress before."

A crowd had formed now and they muttered for Henderson to approve.

"All right. Fine. Three chances."

Priscilla tossed the knife up into the air four times, noting the weight, studying it, memorizing the way it flipped before it came down into her hand. *Now or never...*

She threw the knife up, caught it by the blade, and cast it at the oak.

She missed the entire tree.

But not by much.

She rolled her shoulders, aware the dress had thrown off her aim. She ignored the groaning crowd that seemed to be growing and thanked Private Willoughby for retrieving the knife.

Jaw clamped, she concentrated on the tree and once more threw the knife, this time ready for the unexpected tug of her dress.

The knife lodged in the tree two inches below Henderson's hat. The crowd clapped and whooped.

"She ain't hit it yet," Henderson reminded the audience.

"Yet," Priscilla muttered. In her mind, she felt the blade slip free from her fingers, saw the steel hit the kepi. She could see it. She could feel it. Half the battle.

Priscilla threw the blade. The cast was smooth as warm honey. The blade lodged dead-center in Henderson's kepi and the crowd clapped wildly.

"Dang." Henderson scowled as he marched to the tree, pulled the knife free, retrieved his hat, and poked his finger through the hole. "Now what am I supposed to do?"

"Again," a man in the crowd behind Priscilla called. "Do it again."

"I need a target."

Handkerchiefs waved at her and found their way to the tree. Still scowling, Henderson handed her the knife. After several throws, all of which Priscilla made, a young lady offered to set her reticule on the side of the wagon.

"I hate to put a hole in your purse, ma'am."

"Oh, it's all right. What a story I'll have if you hit it."

Priscilla shrugged, surprised by the offering. "All right, if you say so."

The reticule suffered a fatal stab wound, much to the delight of the still-growing crowd. But in the instant the knife left her fingers, Priscilla heard and felt the top of her sleeve rip free from the bodice. As the knife hit the target, she slapped her hand over the tear and touched skin.

"Oh, no," she whispered. *Won't Miss Danielle Quartermaine just love this?*

"Don't worry, Priscilla," Bea said, quickly examining the damage. "I think I can fix that. She'll never know."

"All right, well, we're done here then. I can't risk anything else happening to this dress."

Bea's gaze flicked over to Willoughby and back to Priscilla. "Can I try once? Just once?"

Priscilla knew the girl wanted to impress her soldier. What could it hurt? "Okay. Be careful. Take a couple of practice throws."

She missed her first one, but the crowd cheered and clapped encouragement for her.

"Come on, Bea," Priscilla nudged. "You can get it."

Bea missed the next two throws, but the crowd clapped a little louder each time because the knife got a little closer each time. She was whittling down the errors, and Priscilla had every confidence in the girl. "You've got this, Bea."

"Come on, Bea," Private Willoughby said, grinning. "I bet you can hit it."

Bea took a deep breath, stared at the purse on the edge of the wagon bed, exhaled slowly, and tossed the knife. It sank into the reticule and knocked it down inside the wagon. Bea jumped and cheered and grasped hands with Priscilla—then they both froze.

The crowd hadn't uttered a peep.

CHAPTER 19

SKYLER WAS THUNDERSTRUCK. PRISCILLA AND HIS DAUGHTER were throwing knives for the entertainment of the crowd like a pair of gypsies in a carnival. Around him, soldiers were betting on the outcome.

On his daughter.

The utter...the utter *vulgarity* of it infuriated him.

Were it possible, he would have spit nails and breathed fire. "What's next, ladies?"

The two girls turned to him, wide-eyed, sheepish, terrified.

Good. "Will there be arm wrestling? Or perhaps ye'll be boxing next?"

Priscilla straightened and took a step toward him. "Now, don't get so riled, Captain—"

"Riled," he thundered. "I dinnae think it possible to be anymore *riled*, Miss Jones. I'm deeply disappointed in ye both out here carrying on like-like..."

The woman inched forward and narrowed her eyes. "Like what?"

Silence smothered the crowd as the two of them glared

at one another. It was a stunned, mournful silence. He felt the sadness in it but couldn't shake free of it. "Both of ye get home. Lieutenant Owens," he said over his shoulder, "escort them, please."

Nate emerged from the crowd instantly. Had he been watching this fiasco?

"Yes, sir." He hurried over to Priscilla and Bea. "I think we should go, ladies."

Skyler turned toward the crowd. "The rest of ye, the gala is over. Good night."

Lord Corbett broke out of the audience, which was turning to go back inside and ostensibly get coats or other personal belongings. He stormed up to his son. "It's not yer place to end this. And those girls weren't doing anything wrong."

"It was beneath them," he yelled, then lowered his voice to a harsh whisper. "I'm the commanding officer, and tomorrow, I'm taking a patrol out. Take them to Montana with ye."

"Son..."

"Do that for me."

His father looked up at the sky, the ground, the disappearing crowd, and then finally nodded. "Aye."

PRISCILLA WAS mad enough to cry and humiliated enough to crawl into a cave and stay there. She was working her way out of Miss Quartermaine's dress when the front door slammed shut downstairs. Multiple footfalls echoed up the steps. To her surprise, someone stopped at her door and knocked.

Wondering if it was Captain Corbett, hoping it was, hoping he had come to apologize, she flung open the door.

Miss Quartermaine grinned slyly. "I came to check on you. Such an ugly scene. Are you all right?"

Priscilla didn't hear even a speck of concern in the woman's voice. Resolved to the salt Miss Quartermaine would no doubt pour into her wound, she pointed at the damaged shoulder. "I'm sorry. I guess I threw a little too hard. I'll pay you for it."

Miss Quartermaine reached up and rested her hand on Priscilla's cheek. "My dear, adorable friend. It was so worth it."

She turned and was sashaying out the door when Bea appeared. Miss Quartermaine patted her on the head dismissively and went on her way. Priscilla could see the steam come out of Bea's ears.

"Oh, that woman. I hat—"

"Don't say it. Hate is a strong word and it's hard to take back. Love your enemies."

Bea sagged with the correction and ambled over to Priscilla. "Want me to help you get out of it?"

"Yes, please."

She turned around so the girl could free the one hundred infuriating buttons down the back. "Your pa was soooome mad." She wagged her head back and forth. "Let us have it. Let me have it."

"I know. He was acting like we were back behind the church chewing tobacco or—"

"Acting the fool. It reflects on him. I sort of figured he wouldn't approve. I should have stuck with the feeling."

"He's so...so..."

Before they could figure out what was the right word for Captain Corbett, a gentle knock sounded on Priscilla's door. "Miss Jones, may I speak with ye?"

Lord Corbett? Priscilla and Bea exchanged troubled

glances. Bea quickly put a few buttons back as she called, "Just a moment, Grand Da."

More presentable, Priscilla answered the door. "Yes, sir."

The big man hemmed and hawed, scratched his jaw. "Um, well, I'm glad Bea's here." He rocked on his heels and finally sighed. "May I come in?"

Priscilla ushered him in.

"I don't quite know how to say this. I'm troubled by my son's behavior, but I've given my word to honor a request."

A sinking feeling hit Priscilla.

"Miss Jones, I'm so sorry. I thought I'd heard from the Lord on this situation and all I've done is make a fine mess."

The room fell so quiet that Priscilla heard Bea swallow. "Grand Da, what is it?"

"Yer da wants me to take ye both back to Montana with me."

Bea gasped. "That's not bad. I'd love to see your ranch again. I was just a child the last time we were there."

"Aye, a wee bairn ye were."

Priscilla couldn't quite take in the meaning of the announcement. "He wants *me* to leave. Is that it? In which case, Lord Corbett, I'd prefer to head back to Ocoee. I don't have the farm anymore, but I've got the money to buy another. Or maybe I'll travel—"

"Miss Jones..." Lord Corbett hooked his thumbs in his vest pockets and paced the room. "First, ye must know ye're more than welcome at my place. I think ye'd like it, in fact. Montana is wild and free...and I think ye've the disposition to handle it."

"Thank you, but—"

"Skyler has to fight some demons, ladies. One of which is this vile renegade, whom he's going after tomorrow, but he has personal demons. I believe the time away from ye would do him good. Why don't ye both come to Montana with me and stay as long as ye like? I'd love the company of two very fine young ladies, such as yerselves."

"I'd like to sleep on it and pray on it," Priscilla said, being as honest as she knew how.

"By all means. There's only one problem. I'm leaving in the morning."

～

LONG AFTER THE house fell silent, Priscilla lay awake praying. She could get no peace on either leaving for home or going to Montana. Frustrated with herself for not having the ears to hear, she got up, grabbed her robe, and headed to the porch for a little fresh air.

She stepped down to the walkway and stared up at the night sky filled with twinkling, glimmering stars. The fort was quiet, nearly silent. A coyote howled far out on the prairie somewhere, his cry barely making it over the fort wall.

"What is it you want me to do, Lord? Honestly, this has been the hardest thing you've ever asked of me. Captain Corbett is no picnic. I've never known anybody who could hurt my feelings the way he can. Yet, one kind word and I'm floating on clouds. He scares me. The way he makes me feel scares me. I want to go home."

She stood quietly for a long time, waiting, trying to be still and hear his voice. Quietly in her soul, the Lord whispered, *And be not conformed to this world: but be ye transformed by the renewing of your mind.*

She didn't see how that answered any of her questions or stilled her fears.

Then, as if explaining to a child, the words from Shakespeare crossed her mind. *To thine own self be true.*

Priscilla knew there were answers here, but she couldn't

pull them out of the darkness. "I'll sleep on it, Lord. Maybe in the morning, I'll understand."

SKYLER FROZE and sunk deeper into the rocking chair hidden in the shadows on the porch, Darby napping on his lap. He knew he should have made his presence known when Priscilla walked out, but something kept him silent. She prayed or, more accurately, fussed at the Lord—not surprising—with passion that humbled him.

Then she admitted Skyler frightened her. And she frightened him, though he was loathe to admit that to anyone but himself. He had the urge to massage his temples in frustration but didn't move a muscle until she went back inside.

She was going to sleep on the matter. Would she leave with Da?

Bea needed to go, this much he knew. Not just to Da's ranch for the summer, but it was time for her to go someplace safe and civilized. She was coming into her independence as a woman, and he couldn't keep an eye on her every second.

Miss Jones was even more headstrong and independent than Bea. The two of them together would age him before his time. "Aye, Lord, answer her prayer. Let her go home. Take them both out of my hand."

They were never in your hand...

The still, small voice brought him up short. He considered the argument, wrestled with it. He was a soldier, a warrior, a guardian. He protected those he loved. He'd failed Louisa. He would not fail Bea and Priscilla.

He spun on his heel and went back into the house.

CHAPTER 20

"It won't be for long, Bea." Skyler held his daughter in a big, warm hug. "I need to run this renegade to ground and then ye can come back and I won't be so distracted." The lie stung.

"All right, Da. I understand, and I don't mind. I love Grand Da. Besides, this is better than going back East to school."

He hid a flinch by pinching her nose. "Behave, or I still may." He looked past her to the stairs. "Where the devil is Miss Jones?"

"Be right down," she called.

And momentarily, the woman bounced down the steps in her buckskin britches and moccasins, her knife on one hip, a .45 on the other, a rifle in her hand. Skyler literally took a step back in shock. "What are ye doing?"

"I'm going with you."

"No. Ye're not," he said slowly, wondering if he'd heard her correctly.

Priscilla stomped up to him. "Ever since I got here, I've

been trying to conform to your idea of a lady. Well, I'm no Miss Quartermaine, and you're low on scouts."

"Out," Nate said flatly from the doorway.

They both cut their eyes at his interruption. He stepped over the threshold but held the door open, as if he might have to retreat quickly. "We're out of scouts. Sharp Nose, Lone Buffalo, Henry Little Bull. They haven't returned."

"Fort Lowell was sending scouts," Skyler reminded him.

"They haven't arrived, either. I suspect One-Who-Cries has either found them or got word to them to desert."

Skyler bit down on a curse. "We'll go without them. If the scouts show up from Fort Lowell, send them on. If they're scouts, they'll find us."

"I said I'm going with you." Priscilla scrambled to get directly in front of Skyler. "Ignoring me won't make me go away."

"Ye're daft, woman. Go to Montana with my father, or to the devil, but ye'll not ride with a patrol after a savage Indian."

"Skyler..."

He looked over the top of Priscilla's head and glared at Nate, incensed by his soft, insistent voice.

"Can I see you outside for a moment, Captain?"

"I dinnae have time—"

"Captain."

Skyler growled his disgust and stomped out to the porch. Nate followed and gently closed the door behind them. "We don't have any scouts, and she's capable."

"Are ye mad?" Skyler was sure his friend had gone insane if he thought this was a good idea.

"She scouted for the militia back in Ocoee. She understands the situation, the danger. At the first sign of trouble, send her to the rear."

Skyler spun away from him and slapped a porch post. "This is madness. Ye've all lost yer minds."

"Maybe it's why she's here."

The bullet wound on his side twinged and he touched it reflexively. "What do ye mean?"

It took Nate a moment to answer. "God has a plan, Skyler. For all of us. We're here together, now. It's no accident."

"It's too dangerous." He whirled on his friend, finally willing to articulate his fear aloud. "I'll not have another woman I care about die in this godforsaken wilderness."

Nate's brow rose at Skyler's admission, then his face softened and he regarded his old friend with compassion. "You think if you'd taken a command in Washington or Atlanta, Louisa would still be alive?"

"I dragged Louisa out here. It was no place for her. No place for Bea. I couldn't let her go at first, but now I know it's best."

Nate pinched his brow, struggled with something, then patted the air with his hands. "One problem at a time. We need a scout. One-Who-Cries is somewhere in the Defiance area. The closest he's been. We can't let him slip away again, Skyler."

Skyler stubbornly held his peace.

Nate pushed. "You've got to think past your prejudice... and your fear."

Skyler shook his head and let a growl escape that suddenly turned into a word. "Fine."

PRISCILLA PULLED her bandana up over her face, and her hat a little lower to block the dust. Blinking away dry eyes, she glanced over her shoulder. A line of fifty soldiers on horseback rode in perfect military formation, two-by-two. If they were scandalized by her presence, appearance, or the fact she wasn't riding sidesaddle, none of them had let it show.

"Miss Jones, I hope I have impressed upon ye the ferocity of One-Who-Cries." Captain Corbett looked over at her, his gaze hard, determined, but Priscilla saw the fear. He was worried about her, and it caused a pang of guilt.

But she'd prayed and had peace about being here. "The battle is the Lord's, Captain. I'm sure of it."

She'd expected an angry retort. Instead, he said simply, "I hope ye're right."

"Rider coming." They both looked at Nate, who pointed off to the right. A soldier was heading toward them at a full gallop. Skyler raised his hand and the column stopped. The rider skidded to a stop at his side and handed him a dispatch.

Skyler's expression darkened as he read. "One-Who-Cries has taken two more White women hostage. He was last seen in the area of Redemption Pass."

"Redemption Pass," Nate repeated. "He's trading the women?"

"Aye, most likely. Which means there are other players on the stage." He cut his eyes at Priscilla. "And we don't know where or who they are."

She nodded, understanding the warning, and she would heed it. "Let's get in the vicinity of this Redemption Pass and make camp. Then I'll do what I came to do."

FIFTY MEN MADE a lot of noise, even if they were trying not to. The process of bivouacking in a thin forest of pines and cedars simply could not be done without some noise. Men muttered, horses grumbled, rifles clinked, saddles thudded on the ground. Priscilla had tied her horse to a twisted cedar and spent the last twenty minutes staring out over a ledge. The view of the valley beyond was helpful in getting her bearings.

She heard footsteps behind her and the sound sent an unwanted thrill up her spine. "This is a good spot for camp," she said matter-of-factly. "It's high ground, but I'll double-check the ridge up there before I head toward Redemption Pass."

"Aye." Skyler stepped up beside her and pointed. "On the other side of that ridge—that's Redemption Pass. I've ordered a cold camp. No fire. If they don't know we're about, we might spot them before they see us."

She was listening, but she was also studying the valley, the trails, and the streams before she lost the daylight. "I'll find them for ya."

He looked down at the ground, hands resting on his hips. "I...I want ye to be careful."

"I was sort of planning on it." She offered him a little half-smile.

He returned it, but it was a sickly imitation. "I cannae tell you how bad an idea this is."

"Skyler," she turned to him and touched his sleeve. She was surprised at herself for using his name, for touching him, but now that she wasn't trying to be anybody but herself, her confidence had returned. "They'll never see me. They'll never know I was there. I'll come back with every-thing you need to find this Indian and stop him."

"Keep yer hat on. That hair is a beacon."

She touched the end of her braid. "You worry too much."

"Possibly."

The air between them charged with something Priscilla couldn't define. Not electricity, exactly, but just as real, and it gave her goose bumps. Or was it the way he looked at her, his eyes a smoldering, inviting shade of blue? His gaze felt like an honest-to-God caress.

And then he reached out and touched her cheek. Lightning zinged through her whole body. Priscilla's heart hammered so hard in her chest she thought the whole camp could hear it.

"Back before dawn," he said firmly. "If ye're not here, we'll come looking."

Her mouth was open. She shut it and licked her lips. "Nothing'll stop me." *From getting back to you...Lord, please, make sure I get back.*

He lowered his hand and stepped away from her with a curt nod. "Godspeed."

Her legs felt a little wobbly, but when she turned to her horse, everything faded away except the task before her. She stepped into the saddle, gave him a quick look—all she would allow herself—and then nudged her horse off into the forest.

DEAR GOD, what have I done?

Skyler sensed a presence beside him and glanced over at Nate, who was also watching Priscilla head off into the shadowy forest of pines and rocks, the light on the edge of dusk.

"When that girl gets back, you should marry her."

"If she gets back."

CHAPTER 21

THE SENSE THAT SKYLER HAD MADE A TERRIBLE MISTAKE ONLY grew with each passing second of Priscilla's absence. As twilight waged war with dusk, the writhing fear in his gut grew stronger, more insistent. He paced alone near the ledge, watching the valley below for signs of life—a flicker of a campfire, movement in the shadows. He argued that between him and Priscilla, she would most certainly be the one to hear the voice of the Lord, as she said she had.

He stopped abruptly and waited. He didn't know for what. He exhaled softly...and listened.

Stop her.

An order from a Superior Officer snapped his head up and he reacted instantly, without questioning it. He rushed to his own horse, unwound its reins from the picket line, and raced after Priscilla. She couldn't be far. She'd only been gone a few minutes.

In less than five, he spotted her winding her way up the trail between some boulders. He pounded toward her, his horse's hooves echoing like thunder on the hard ground.

Priscilla heard and spun around. Skyler could see the glare on her face, even in the low light.

"What in the Sam Hill are you doing?" she whispered as he rode up to her. "Trying to get me killed? I could hear you—"

"Back to camp." He spun his nervous, prancing mount in a circle. "Now."

"What? Why?"

"It's an order. That's all ye need to hear."

Before she could argue, a shot rang out from behind them at the camp, followed by a wild, erratic volley of gunfire. He and Priscilla bolted toward the firefight without another word.

FROM THE COVER OF TREES, Skyler and Priscilla paused to assess the skirmish. Flashes of fire revealed the enemy's position. Apparently several men had taken a position in a narrow grouping of rocks just above the soldiers. They had high ground, some cover in the boulders, but no room to maneuver. Below, Skyler's men were shooting back and scrambling for protection behind trees, rocks, even horses.

Nate was shouting orders, but Skyler couldn't hear him. The smoke and descending darkness were beginning to fog the battlefield. His mind raced over the strategies. "Flank them." He looked at Priscilla. "It's only the two of us, but if we can draw their fire, Nate may have time to attempt a charge." *Or charge and flank them on the other side with more men.*

Without a moment's hesitation, she snatched her rifle free, leaped from the saddle, and headed for a rock up the hill. Skyler followed. In seconds, they had established their own cover behind boulders, tracked the flashes of gunfire, and picked their targets. Rifles roared, and bullets whizzed all around them. Chunks of rock rained down on them.

Cries of pain drifted through the smoke. Skyler prayed the sounds did not come from any of his men. He shot at a flash of muzzle fire. Who were they fighting? The volley continued for several minutes. Out of ammunition in both her revolver and her gun belt, Priscilla raised her rifle.

Skyler emptied one Colt, then the second. Now he and Priscilla were using rifles. Another, faster volley of fire from a slightly different location told him Nate had split the men and some were attempting the flanking maneuver.

A bullet ricocheted off the sandstone next to Skyler's head and he turned. Fire flashed from a boulder. "They're behind us," he yelled, taking a shot at shadowy movement.

Priscilla spun, surveyed the area in an instant, and fired as well. A man yelled and fell from behind the rock. Somehow, Skyler and Priscilla wound up back-to-back, shooting at anything that moved. Men were firing, but the gunfire was moving away.

"They're retreating."

A bugle sounded from below, followed by the thunder of hooves. Full darkness had fallen now, but a few more shots echoed, then silence. Skyler cocked his rifle and listened, his finger on the trigger. A few groans drifted through the smoky air, but the battle was over.

"Let's get down there, find Nate."

Skyler led the way, Priscilla riding close behind. His mind was on high alert, every sound a potential threat. Battle keen, eyes wide, he still had the presence of mind to marvel over her courage, strength, and steady hand.

As the pair wound their way down the rocky hill, he noted the shadowy shapes of bodies in the rocks. Bursting into the camp, he called for Nate. Sergeant Bonhoffer limped up, holding a bloodied arm. "He took some men and went after them, Captain."

"All right, gather up the wounded. Reestablish the perimeter. Get me a report of casualties. I need ten men to mount up and we'll go after Lieutenant Owens."

Priscilla, who had not dismounted, straightened in the saddle, ready to go, Skyler noted with admiration. As the soldiers were hastening to follow orders, the small contingent re-entered camp, Nate in the lead. "Captain." He trotted over and dismounted wearily.

"Report. What happened here?"

"Apparently a band of some twenty Mexicans were in the area. Saw us coming and hid in the rocks. I split our force as quickly as I could and managed a two-pronged charge up the middle and to their right flank. I noted there was already someone firing on their left flank and we took advantage of their distraction. No survivors."

Skyler was proud of his friend and slapped him on the shoulder. "Good job, lieutenant."

"Sir," Sergeant Bonhoeffer interrupted. "No casualties. Two men are hurt pretty badly, though."

"Very well. We'll do a night march. Get off this mountain and back to the fort by dawn. Get a detail to bury the bodies." He turned to the darkness of the forest and sighed with exhaustion. "One-Who-Cries will have to wait...one more day."

CHAPTER 22

EXHAUSTED, DUSTY, THINKING WITH DIFFICULTY, LIKE THE
gears in her head had rusted, Priscilla sat down on Skyler's
settee. The house was so quiet. Then she remembered Bea
must have left with Lord Corbett. She would miss them
both.

She shook her head, trying to shake loose the sludge of
heavy fatigue. So much had happened in the last forty-eight
hours. It was all a blur of the sulfur smell of gun smoke and
the piercing crack of rifles. She'd never been in a battle.
She'd fought one Indian one time on her own, but he hadn't
expected her to have a knife. It hadn't ended well for him.
Still, she regretted taking a life. Last night, she thought she'd
hit two, maybe three men. From a distance, death wasn't so
jarring.

Afterward, on their way back, the lull of the swaying
saddle rocking her in and out of sleep, she had time to
think, to recall the battle. She thought of standing with
Skyler, fighting beside him. It seemed the thing a woman
should do for her man. *A* man, she corrected.

But it was more than that. She'd been fighting for his

life, and something told her he'd been fighting for hers. What a pair they made. If only he could see past her countrified speech and lack of knowledge of table settings.

She slumped on the couch. "I shouldn't think so much right now," she whispered to the Lord. "I'll get sad. I should sleep and deal with everything tom—"

"Miss Jones, what a pleasant surprise."

She's still here? Priscilla had darn near forgotten about Miss Danielle Quartermaine. She dragged her gaze up to greet the woman, who was fresh as a spring daisy in her flowing dress of pink paisley. "Is it?" was all Priscilla could manage.

"Of course it is. But I was looking for Skyler."

"I reckon he's still at the office. Something about new dispatches." Priscilla had been too tired to catch all the details.

"Well, as long as he's not here..." Miss Quartermaine sashayed a little closer. "I heard..." She scanned Priscilla's bedraggled appearance from top to bottom and laid a hand on her heart. "Oh, my, I guess the rumors are true."

"Rumors?"

"I heard you rode out of the fort in your frontier clothing, a gun on your hip and one in your saddle. Quite the pioneer woman, aren't you?"

"Miss Quartermaine, if you've got something to say, I sure would appreciate it if you'd get to it. I'm just a little tired."

"Oh, I had no point, really. I'm just amazed that you thought a woman of your...breeding and background could entangle a man like Captain Corbett. I find it amusing, is all."

Priscilla sparked a little to the comment about her background and breeding. After all, that was an insult to Ma and

Pa, but fussing with this highfalutin, snooty, know-it-all would avail nothing. "I appreciate your view on things."

"As do I."

Both women startled at Skyler's voice. Priscilla sat up but didn't rise. Miss Quartermaine spun round to the captain and adopted a sweet, inviting smile. "Skyler, I was looking for you."

"Aye, ye found me." He stepped away from the door but left it open. "Now ye can leave."

Priscilla dropped her gaze to the floor, embarrassed for the woman.

"That was rather rude," Miss Quartermaine pointed out in a hurt, surprised tone.

"Forgive me." He sighed. "I'm tired. And I've been a fool. If ye'd be so kind as to leave, I need to have a word with Miss Jones."

The tension in the air was as thick as fog on the Blue Ridge. Miss Quartermaine laced her fingers over her stomach, shot a cold glare at Priscilla, but then nodded sweetly at Skyler. "Certainly. Perhaps I'll see you for dinner?"

"I dinnae think so, Danielle."

The woman's jaw tightened like she could bite through barbed wire. "I see." Without another word, she left, holding her skirt and her chin up. A nervous silence in the house followed her exit.

Priscilla's heart trip-hammered in her chest. Her pulse rocketed into the heavens. Her breathing became shallow. She almost stopped altogether when Skyler sat down beside her. Suddenly, Priscilla felt too light-headed to speak and she couldn't look at him. Had he come to bid her goodbye, as well?

He cleared his throat, started to speak, bit it back. Another few seconds passed before he tried again. He sighed, a frustrated sound, and ran a hand through his dirty, caramel hair.

Priscilla sneaked a look over at him. "You all right?"

"Nae. I am not." He rose, paced the room. Priscilla watched him, owl-eyed and befuddled.

"Priscilla, I have been an unforgivable fool and a snob."

She was inclined to agree but refrained from voicing it. He'd called her by her first name and it elated her.

He shook his head and came back to join her on the settee. He sighed again, like a man defeated. "The first thing I must know..." He turned to her, and the pleading in his gaze, like a child caught with his hand in the cookie jar, froze her in place. "I must know if ye can forgive me."

At least the question wasn't a difficult one. "Aye," she said softly, smiling at him.

He exhaled, as if he'd just released a heavy burden. "I dinnae deserve it."

"I don't deserve what Jesus did for me. How can I hold other people's sins against them? I'm commanded to love and forgive."

"I need ye to forgive me for more than that reason. More than a commandment."

"Because I want to forgive you?"

"Aye."

"Skyler, I..." She stared down at her hands, toyed with a chipped fingernail. "I forgave you the moment you said I looked beautiful in my gown."

Their eyes met. He touched her cheek. "Lass, I fell in love with ye when I saw ye at dinner in yer ridiculous bare feet."

She gasped. *He loves me, Lord? He loves me?* Priscilla laughed and somehow it turned into a near sob of relief and joy, but she bit down on her lip to keep it under control.

"Louisa...her death has weighed on me. I blamed myself for bringing her to a place she was nae equipped for. And

Bea, she's growing up now, beyond my control. I was going to send her to a school back East."

"But...?"

"I was thinking back. Ye've taught my daughter to throw knives." He blinked and shook his head, as if he couldn't believe those words came out of his mouth. "Knives. And then ye and I, when we were standing, fighting together... yer courage...ye...uh." He struggled for words. "I guess what I'm trying to say is, ye've shown me a woman can be strong, brave, someone to depend on. Some are a flower that's watered and kept lovely but they're fragile. Ye're not fragile."

Priscilla wished for words but, having only hope to his meaning, merely nodded.

"And what I'm getting to, after a laborious few minutes..." He slipped to one knee and took Priscilla's hand in his. "Will ye marry me, Priscilla Jones? Marry me and stay with Bea and me?"

A dam broke in Priscilla's heart and the tears spilled down her cheeks. He loved her. For who she was. "What about my buckskins and my britches?"

"Wear them, lass. Wear them every day, everywhere if it pleases ye, and pound the fool who comments on them."

She laughed and wiped away the tears. "Pa made me promise him something, and I intend to stick to it."

"And what's that?"

"He said, 'You marry this captain. You make him a good wife. And you have a passel of fine, healthy children.' And he asked me to tell them about him."

"Yer father was a good and wise man...but I wouldn't want ye to say yes to me simply out of a promise to him."

She reached out and drifted fingers across his stubbly cheek. "I'm head-over-heels for you, Captain Skyler Corbett. All out, knocked-down, drunk-in-love with you."

A slow smile spread on his lips and then he pressed

those lips to Priscilla's and she nearly fainted dead away at his gentle, warm touch. Eyes closed, new sensations and unfathomable emotions roared to life in her, set her skin on fire. Oh, but it wasn't painful. She wanted to feel this way forever.

Without breaking the kiss, Skyler pulled her to her feet and wrapped his arms around her. His lips devoured hers and then he deepened the kiss and Priscilla did cease to breathe. She could only feel, only dream of the future, but not one rational thought resided in her head.

Skyler drifted his lips over her cheek, down her jawline, across her throat, back to her lips. "I've one request, lass, if ye'll honor it."

Priscilla couldn't think of a thing to which she'd say no. "Name it." Was that her voice, so dreamy and soft?

"Wear a dress for me once in a while?"

EPILOGUE

Dear Father,

You'll be pleased to know, after much kicking and screaming, Captain Corbett has, indeed, taken Ocoee's little wild cat to wife.

There were moments when Lord Corbett and I both thought the plan would fail, but we never should have doubted. The Lord was in this.

We all agreed we'd heard from Him. But, oh, we of little faith. I'm sorry I ever doubted Him or you.

Miss Jones paints lovely pictures of the landscape as a peaceful pastime. She is also teaching the men to throw knives. The champion, however, is Bea, Captain Corbett's daughter. She is undefeated thus far in the season.

As far as Miss Jones's attire, on Sundays and special occasions, she does, as she promised, wear a dress. Occasionally, even for no reason at all. Captain Corbett has adapted, putting away his prejudice because he knows he's got the better end of the bargain—a wife who can cook, sew, and fight and shoot.

If the residents of Ocoee can spare their doctor for a bit, we'd love to have you visit with us at the fort. Please know that I miss you, Father.

Write soon.

Love,

Your son, Nate

AFTERWORD

Priscilla Jones is a tribute to the following real, wildly courageous pioneer women:

She is an amalgamation. She is the young, determined wife of a fallen American soldier manning his cannon at the Battle of Monmouth, Mary Hays. She is the frontiersman's wife whose temper the Cherokee so feared they named her War Woman, Nancy Morgan Hart. She is the sassy young actress who wasn't afraid of anything, not even the mud and snow of the Klondike, Kate Rockwell. She is the rancher's wife who lived isolated and alone on the windswept Montana prairie, Nannie Alerdson.

These women personified *never give up, never back down, never lose faith.*

God bless America and her sassy daughters.

A LOOK AT: HELL-BENT ON BLESSINGS

Left bankrupt and homeless by a worthless husband, Harriet Pullen isn't about to lay down and die.

Finding a temporary home for her children, she heads to the gold rush town of Blessings, California to start life over. One carefully planned step at a time, she's going to make a home for her family, regain her financial independence, and build a new ranch—bigger and better than the one she lost. God help the man who ever gets in her way again.

Jason Meredith, an old friend, has a few things he'd like to say to Harriet, especially now that she's a widow. He might have better luck surviving a bear attack, though, than thawing her frozen heart. He's got his work cut out for him, but Jason's a patient man. At least, he used to think he was...

AVAILABLE SEPTEMBER 2025

ABOUT THE AUTHOR

Heather Blanton is a *USA Today* bestselling author of thirty Christian Western romances, including the highly rated and awarded Romance in the Rockies series. She is also an award-winning script writer. Her Romance in the Rockies series has been optioned for a limited TV series, and her script *Unbridled Hearts* is currently optioned as well.

She grew up in the mountains of Western North Carolina on a steady diet of *Bonanza, Gunsmoke,* and John Wayne Westerns. Her daddy taught her to shoot when she was five, and she can hit that at which she aims.

Her novels are all Christian Western romance because she enjoys creating feisty pioneer women who struggle to find love and hold on to their faith. Like all good, old-fashioned Westerns, there is always justice, a moral message, American values, lots of high adventure, unexpected plot twists, and often a touch of suspense.

www.authorheatherblanton.com